ADAM CHRISTOPHER

KILLING IS MY BUSINESS

THE LA TRILOGY — BOOK II

TITANBOOKS

Killing is My Business
Print edition ISBN: 9781783296910
E-book edition ISBN: 9781783296880

Published by Titan Books
A division of Titan Publishing Group Ltd
144 Southwark Street, London SE1 0UP

First edition: July 2017
2 4 6 8 10 9 7 5 3 1

This is a work of fiction. Names, characters, places, and incidents either are the product of the author's imagination or are used fictitiously, and any resemblance to actual persons, living or dead, business establishments, events, or locales is entirely coincidental. The publisher does not have any control over and does not assume any responsibility for author or third-party websites or their content.

A CIP catalogue record for this title is available from the British Library.

Printed and bound in Great Britain by CPI Group Ltd.

Did you enjoy this book? We love to hear from our readers. Please email us at: readerfeedback@titanemail.com, or write to us at the above address.

To receive advance information, news, competitions, and exclusive offers online, please sign up for the Titan newsletter on our website.
www.titanbooks.com

For Sandra, always.

And for Mitzy, forever.

Did you ever read what they call Science Fiction?
It's a scream. It is written like this . . .

—*Raymond Chandler*
March 14, 1953

KILLING IS MY BUSINESS

1

Listen to this:

Vaughan Delaney was a planner for the city of Los Angeles. He occupied a position high enough up the ladder that entitled him to an office at an equally high altitude in a tall building downtown that was home to a number of other local government desks. The office came with a salary that was high for a city employee but nothing to write a favorite uncle about, and a view that was simply to die for.

Vaughan Delaney was forty-two years old and he liked suits that were a light blue-gray in color. He carried a buckskin briefcase that wasn't so much battered as nicely worn in. On his head he liked to position a fedora that was several shades darker than his suit. The hat had a brim that looked at first glance to be a little wide for the kind of hat that a city planner would wear, but Vaughan Delaney did not break the rules, neither in his job nor in his private life.

He had a position a lot of people envied, along with the life that went along with it, and he stuck rigidly within the boundaries of both.

Actually, that wasn't quite true. Because the one thing that didn't fit Vaughan Delaney was his car.

His car was a 1957 Plymouth Fury, a mobile work of art in red and white with enough chrome to blind oncoming traffic on the bright and sunny mornings that were not uncommon in this part of California. The machine had fins like you wouldn't believe and when the brake lights lit you'd think they were rocket motors. It was the kind of car you could fly to the moon in, only when you got to the moon you'd cast one eye on the fuel gauge and you'd pat the wheel with your kidskin-gloved hand, admiring the fuel economy as you pointed the scarlet hood off somewhere toward Jupiter and pressed the loud pedal.

It was a great car and it was in perfect shape. Factory fresh. It was getting on for ten years old but Vaughan Delaney had looked after it well.

And, I had to admit, that car caught my optics. It wasn't jealousy—I liked my own car well enough, a Buick that was a satisfying ride, functional and elegant and with a few optional extras you wouldn't find outside a science laboratory.

No, what I had for the red Plymouth Fury was something else. Admiration, and admiration for Vaughan Delaney too. He was every element the city man but that car was a jackrabbit. Perhaps it was his mid-life crisis. Perhaps he was telling the city to go take a jump while he sat shuffling papers in his nice office with his sensible suit and practical hat. Look what I get to drive to the office in the morning, he said. Look what I get to drive out to lunch every

Wednesday. Look what I get to drive home in the evening. It was the kind of car that people would lean out of the office windows to take a look at, and Vaughan Delaney did every bit to help, the way he parked the red-and-white lightning bolt right outside the office door.

Because Vaughan Delaney had reached a certain level within the city hierarchy that allowed him to pick his own secretary based on the color of her hair and the length of her skirt and he was not a man who had to walk very far from his car to his desk.

He was also a family man. When the Plymouth Fury wasn't outside the office or being driven to lunch on Wednesdays it lived in a two-car garage that sat next to a modest but modern bungalow in Gray Lake. Next to the Fury was commonly parked a yellow vehicle that General Motors had shooed out the door without much of a fuss, a rectangular lozenge on wheels with whitewall tires shining and seat belt tight and the sense of humor removed for safety reasons.

This was not a car to take much of an interest in. It belonged to Vaughan Delaney's wife. Her name was Cindy Delaney.

Cindy Delaney loved her husband and let him know by kissing him on the cheek each and every morning before her husband went to work. The children loved him too. There were two of those, a boy and a girl, and both of them had blond hair like their mother and they were both a decade shy of joining the army and both of them kissed their father on the cheek each and every morning like their mother did, the only difference being that Vaughan Delaney had to go down on one knee so they could smell his aftershave. Then he blasted off in the Plymouth Fury and the quiet street in Gray Lake was quiet once more until Cindy Delaney took the children to school in the yellow boat and then came back again twenty minutes later. Then she put on a housecoat to keep her dress clean and she drove a vacuum over the bungalow while her husband drove a desk down in the city.

They were a nice family. Middle class, middle income, middle ambition. The children would grow up and the boy would play football at high school with his parents watching and the girl would play flute in the school orchestra with her parents watching and all was right with the world.

I knew all of this because I'd been watching Vaughan Delaney for three weeks. I'd been to the street in Gray Lake and had sat in my car and I'd watched life in and around the bungalow. I'd been to the office building downtown and had sat in my car and watched the Plymouth Fury come in for landing and Vaughan Delaney hop, skip, and jump up the stairs into the building and then waltz down the same steps some eight hours later.

Vaughan Delaney looked like a swell guy with a good job and a nice car and a happy family.

It was just a shame that he had to die.

2

It was when Wednesday rolled around for the fourth time that I rolled the Buick into a spot across the street from the downtown office in which Vaughan Delaney parked his blue-suited behind Monday to Friday, nine to five. While the building was owned and operated by the City of Los Angeles, it wasn't actually city hall, which was good because paying a little visit to a target in city hall would have made the job a little more difficult than I would have liked. It wasn't exactly going to be easy here but I had some ideas. I'd been scoping it out for long enough and it was now coming up to eight fifty-five in the morning on the last Wednesday of Vaughan Delaney's life and it was time for me to get to work.

Two minutes after I turned the Buick's engine off the red Plymouth Fury swept into the slot right outside the steps that led up to the front door of the building. The slot wasn't posted as belonging to anyone in particular but it was always free. There was a spot marked for Vaughn Delaney in the parking lot out the back of the building, but that spot had the disadvantage of not being visible from the main street, and Vaughan Delaney was proud of his car and he liked it to be visible.

I knew about the parking lot around back and the slot that was posted for Vaughan Delaney because I'd checked. I'd checked everything there was to check about Vaughan Delaney and that included where he parked his car during the day and during the night and what his lunch habits were.

Lunch was my moment of opportunity. More specifically, lunch on Wednesdays, because Wednesday was the one day a week he poked his head out the office door before five o'clock. On Wednesdays he came out between twelve oh-two and twelve oh-three and he skipped down the office steps with one hand pressing his fedora against his scalp and the other swinging the buckskin briefcase. Then he got into his rocket ship, threw the briefcase on the seat beside him, and blasted off for galaxies unknown before making his re-entry anytime between twelve fifty-five and twelve fifty-six.

Vaughan Delaney was the kind of guy who watched the clock. That was something else I admired about him.

I say "lunch," but that was really a misnomer, given that in the three weeks I'd been following him Vaughan Delaney hadn't done much in the way of eating food, unless he had Cindy Delaney's homemade sandwiches in his buckskin briefcase and he ate with one hand on the wheel. Because what Vaughan Delaney did during Wednesday lunchtimes was *drive*.

The first Wednesday I watched and waited in my own car outside his office. I didn't move it from the spot across the street and I didn't move myself from the driver's seat. I just kept my optics on the office and watched as the city planner came down the stairs and got into the car and drove off and I watched as he drove back and got out of the car and went up the stairs again.

The second Wednesday I followed him and I must have been surprised at what I discovered (although I didn't remember—I never remembered) because all he did was drive in circles around downtown LA, going along East 1st Street until it become West 1st Street and then hooking in Figueroa and then down to Olympic Boulevard and then around and about and back to his office. I kept a good distance but he never got out of my sight. He never stopped for lunch either, and if he was eating on the go then I never saw him do it through the acreage of glass that wrapped around the upper half of his vehicle. The leather seats inside the Plymouth Fury were red and white like the outside of the car and you certainly wouldn't want to spill mayonnaise and ketchup on them. Vaughan Delaney was nothing if not a careful man.

The third Wednesday he fired the boosters on the Fury and he headed into my territory. Hollywood, California. Beverly Boulevard. Highland Avenue. Santa Monica Boulevard. The Plymouth Fury bucked and rocked and weaved. It stopped at lights and I stopped with it. It roared off when the lights changed and I did my best to keep up.

Then he went back to the office and went up the stairs and that was that.

It was interesting but perhaps not remarkable. Maybe he

just liked driving. A car like that, I'd stoke its afterburners once weekly too. Maybe Cindy Delaney's sandwiches were waiting for him in the drawer of his desk.

Vaughan Delaney's Wednesday sightseeing tours gave me an idea. Because one week he'd take off and then . . .

Well, one week he'd take off and he wouldn't come back.

Vaughan Delaney had made my job just that little bit easier and for that I was much obliged. I'd been sitting in my car for too long and I was feeling restless. I didn't know if we were on any kind of timetable but Ada hadn't said anything about it.

Timetables, it had to be said, were not my strong point, given that I had no recollection of events prior to six in the morning, each and every day. That was because I was a robot with a state-of-the-art miniaturized data tape sitting behind my chest plate, a ribbon of condensed magnetic storage slowly winding from one reel to the other, the events of the day recording themselves through the medium of me.

"Day" being the operative word. My memory tape was a technological wonder, but it had a limit. Specifically, a twenty-four-hour limit. Subtract a couple more to allow my batteries to recharge back at the office, and I was down to twenty-two hours of working time. And when I switched back on afterward, the world around me was born anew, the old memory tape boxed and archived and a new clean one installed. I guess I was the one who did the boxing and installing. I don't know. I didn't remember.

So my surveillance of Vaughan Delaney, my three weeks of watching and waiting in my car, of following him on his lunchtime drives around town, my visits to his house in

Gray Lake, my observation of Cindy Delaney and her own daily habits—none of this was anything I could actually recall. Every morning I'd wake up in my alcove in the computer room behind my office and my boss, Ada, would give me a rundown on current jobs. In fact, Ada *was* the computer room, and my alcove was inside her next to her own spinning memory tapes and flashing data banks. All that tape, she had no problem remembering anything at all. Once she'd laid out the details of the current job, including what I had done and what I needed to do, I was out the door with a spring in my step and a few homicidal thoughts fizzing between my voltage amplification coils.

And the current job, singular, for the last three weeks, had been Vaughan Delaney and nothing else. But even if I didn't remember a thing about it, and even though there didn't seem to be any particular kind of timetable supplied by our anonymous client, I figured I'd spent enough time sitting in my car and had better get the job done at some point.

That point was today. Wednesday.

I sat in the car and I watched and I waited. Vaughan Delaney had been in his office for an hour. He wouldn't appear for another two. I sat and I waited. I opened my window an inch and listened to the beat of the city around me.

It was a busy street and the office got a lot of foot traffic, some of which even stopped to admire the car that was the same color as a fire engine parked right outside the door. Back on my side of the street there was a drugstore down on the corner that got a lot of foot traffic too. I watched people come and go and some of those people were carrying brown paper bags. Some people went inside and stayed there, sitting on stools at the bench inside the front window as they drank coffee and ate sandwiches.

I watched them a while longer and then I thought I'd quite like a sandwich and a coffee to pass the time. I didn't need to sit and watch the building. Vaughan Delaney's schedule was as regular as the oscillators in my primary transformer. I had time to spare.

I got out of the car and stood on the sidewalk for a moment, one hand on the driver's door, looking over at the office building. A sandwich and a coffee still felt like a great idea. It was the kind of thing you got when you spent a lot of time waiting and watching. It helped pass the time, like smoking and talking about baseball with the boys and making your own flies for fly-fishing.

Of course, I had no need for a coffee or a sandwich or a cigarette. If I walked down to the drugstore and went inside and bought one of each I wouldn't have any use for them on account of the fact that I didn't eat or drink.

I was a robot.

And still as I stood there in the street the faint memory of the taste of fresh hot coffee tickled the back of my circuits. An echo of another life, maybe. A life that didn't belong to me but that belonged to my creator, Professor Thornton.

A coffee and a sandwich would be a real waste, but maybe the drugstore could sell me something else. Maybe I could get a magazine. A magazine or a paperback book. That sounded fun. I had two hours to kill before I followed the target on his weekly jaunt around the City of Angels.

I closed the door of the car and I pulled my collar up and my hat down and I headed to the drugstore, just a robot minding his own business. Most people in the street minded their own too. So I was a robot. Big deal. The city had been full of robots once. Some people remembered them and some people were too young. Some people glanced at me and held their glance a moment longer than they normally would, but there was some stiff competition coming from the miracle machine parked up on the other side of the street.

I never made it into the drugstore, which was a shame as I was set on the idea of a paperback book. In fact, I never even got close to the corner, because this Wednesday Vaughan Delaney decided to make a change to his routine, and he did this by falling out of the window of his office on the sixth floor of the building and making a splashdown right on the white lid of the red Plymouth Fury.

The crashing sound this unexpected event made was just as loud as if another car had collided with the Plymouth instead of a human body. The initial smash was followed by the slow tinkle of broken glass and more than a couple of screams and shouts from the good folk who had, until that moment, just been minding their business on a sunny midweek morning.

I froze where I was and looked across the street. The car was still rocking on its suspension and the roof had caved in toward the back, bending enough for the rear windshield to shatter. The front windshield remained intact, most likely due to its prodigious expanse of curved glass, which clearly added a great deal of strength to the structure.

Vaughan Delaney lay in the concave roof, arms and legs spread out like he was getting comfortable in his big bed in Gray Lake after a good night out with the boys in accounting. Said boys were still in the office above the car and were now leaning out and looking down and pointing, as though there was some other direction their former colleague could have gone. I heard more shrieks and sobs from above as the realization spread across the whole office like the blood spreading out from Vaughan Delaney's ruptured insides onto the roof of the car, turning the white leather covering it the same color as the bodywork. Soon enough other windows up and down the whole side of the building and its neighbors opened and more heads looked out. A man in a uniform that marked him out as the concierge ran out of the building and raced to the car fast enough to leave his peaked cap floating down the steps behind him. He was joined by a couple of other men, one of whom had flown off the sidewalk next to me to lend a hand at the scene. Around me people stopped and stared and either turned away with a shudder or a gasp as they dropped their shopping or they just stood there and looked on as they sucked their cigarettes and adjusted their hats.

I didn't have a cigarette to suck but I was wearing a hat and I adjusted it just like everyone else. I stood there and watched as in just a few minutes more people came out of the building and from up and down the street to form a not insubstantial audience around the wrecked car.

I walked back to my own vehicle and got in. I kept my eyes on the scene. Someone in shirtsleeves had climbed up onto the hood of the Plymouth Fury, but on reaching the windshield he'd stopped with his hands on hips like he was unsure of the route ahead.

Sitting between me and the passenger seat in my car was a telephone. It started to ring. I let it ring and I started the car and pulled away and headed up toward Hollywood.

When I was clear of the scene by an intersection or two I picked the phone up.

"Hi," I said.

"What's cooking, Ray?" Ada sounded cheerful as she always did and she sounded like she was pulling on a cigarette which she sometimes did and which I knew to be merely an echo in my circuits of someone else, given that my boss was a computer the size of an office.

"I'm heading back," I said. "Get the coffee on."

"Nice piece of action downtown, Ray."

I frowned, or at least it felt like I frowned. My face was a solid flat plate of bronzed steel-titanium alloy and my mouth was a slot and a grill that was about as mobile as any of the four faces carved onto the side of Mount Rushmore.

"If you're talking about the untimely end of Vaughan Delaney, then I guess that is action of a fashion," I said. "Although I have to ask how you knew about it given that it happened all of three minutes ago."

"Oh, it's all over the place, Ray. Someone called it in to the cops and I just happened to be listening in. Then everybody started calling it in to the cops."

"I did think it was a little early for the late edition."

"It'll be front page tomorrow," said Ada. "Perhaps below the fold. Depends what other standard Hollywood depravity goes on before sundown, I guess." Ada blew smoke around my circuits. "Not your usual style, but you know what I say, whatever works, works."

"Except I had nothing to do with the death of Vaughan Delaney."

"That's good, chief. Keep it up. Deny everything, ask for your phone call, and don't speak until you get a lawyer."

I came up to a set of lights that were red. I'd come several blocks and was at the corner of Beverly and South Union. I didn't like this part of the city. Hollywood might have been crummy but downtown Los Angeles was strange to me, too many tall buildings standing too close to one another. I wouldn't be happy until I was back home.

The lights changed and I kept on in a westerly direction.

"Ada, listen, it wasn't me," I said. "The city planner hit terminal velocity under his own volition."

"Oh."

"Oh?"

"Oh, as in, oh well, accidents happen."

"You don't sound too worried."

"Should I be?"

"Do we still get paid?"

"Well," said Ada, "the target is dead, isn't he?"

"That he is."

"So job done. That was good of Mr. Delaney to do our work for us. Nice and clean is the way I like it."

I made a buzzing sound like a bumblebee trapped under a glass. Ada got the message and she laughed.

"Don't worry about it, chief," she said. "Come back to the office and take the rest of the day off."

I thought again about the paperback book I was going to buy. As I drove I kept an optic out and I hit pay dirt nearly at once.

There was a bookstore on the corner with a Buick-sized space right outside it.

"I'm on my way," I said as I pulled the car up. "I'm just making a little stop first."

"Going for a root beer float, chief?"

I frowned on the inside again and Ada started laughing.

"Go knock yourself out," she said. And then the phone was dead.

When I got out of my car I paused a while in the sunshine of the late morning. I turned and looked at the bookstore, and then I turned and looked down the street in a southeasterly direction. Four miles away Los Angeles city planner Vaughan Delaney was being scooped out of the broken roof of his red-and-white 1957 Plymouth Fury.

Then I swung the door of the Buick closed and I headed into the bookstore with just one thought buzzing around my solenoids.

It sure was a shame about that car.

3

"What kind of car was it again?"

I looked up from my book. In the computer room behind my office Ada's lights flashed and her reel-to-reel tapes spun and I could hear the buzz and the hum and the sound of the second hand on a fast stopwatch ticking ever onward.

"Plymouth Fury," I said. "1957. Red and white. Excellent condition. Not sure what the Blue Book was, but I'd say the value dropped pretty quick this morning."

"Like Vaughan Delaney," said Ada. "That sure is a shame."

"You're telling me."

"Still, I guess the widow could collect on the insurance."

"Car or life?"

"Either or," said Ada. Then her tapes went back to spinning and I went back to my book. On the cover was a man in a silver suit with a fishbowl on his head and next to him was a woman in a chain-mail bikini and nothing else. She had blond hair long enough to touch the rocky ground they were standing on. Above them the sky was black and the man in the space suit was pointing a ray gun at a tentacled monstrosity that was crawling over the horizon. The rocky surface belonged to the planet Aldabaran III and if the man and his alien beauty didn't get back to the safety of his 22 Model Sirus Hardtop then they were going to be in all kinds of trouble.

I was four chapters in and loving every page.

There was a click, and then the reel on one of Ada's mainframes slowed to a halt, then spun up again in the opposite direction. I looked up into the corner of the room where there was nothing but the ceiling and the wall, but for some reason it felt like the spot from which the boss looked down on her employee.

"Something up?" I asked. I folded the corner of the page and closed the book.

"New job," said Ada. "Take a look."

There was a ticker-tape machine built into one of the consoles. It sprang to life. I got up and went over and took a look at what the tape said. There was a name and an address.

"Emerson Ellis." I looked back up into the corner. "Who's Emerson Ellis?"

"That doesn't matter, Ray. You know that."

There was a photographic printer next to the ticker-tape machine. It began to grind. I watched the slot for what felt like a very long time and then a picture poked out and flopped into the wire tray underneath.

I pulled it out and uncurled the edges and took a look. The photograph was of a man with a round face and soft features and a bald head that was surrounded by a halo of dark hair.

"*That's* Emerson Ellis," said Ada. "Now, be a good boy and go pay him a visit."

I put the photograph into my jacket. I picked my hat up off the table and my coat off the back of the door.

And then I went to go and meet Mr. Emerson Ellis.

And I was fairly sure he wasn't going to be very pleased to meet *me*.

4

After a detour or two I finally followed the address on the ticker tape and headed west across town until I could see the shield of the city of Beverly Hills. I found the address quickly on a busy, high-class street lined on one side by offices and on the other with boutiques, both factions engaged in a cold war over how many acres of plate glass window they could fit across their respective frontages to display the quality of their products or the glamor of their clients or customers within.

If I'd been to Beverly Hills before I didn't know it, but already I was planning on making as early a departure as possible.

I drove up and down the street twice and spent what time I'd gained getting there looking for a place to put the car. I found an angled spot around the corner and then I walked back to the address on the ticker tape, surveying the office from across the street. Like all the other addresses on this block it was a wall of glass behind which beehive hairdos and slim-fitting suits moved.

I frowned, on the inside. Before I did a job I liked to watch the scene a while, preferably from the comfort of my car, but having to park around the corner put paid to that.

There was a neon sign reflected in the windows of the office across the street. The sign was green. It didn't flash, because neon signs don't flash in Beverly Hills. But I liked what the sign said.

I turned on my heel and walked into this city's equivalent of a corner drugstore. A few minutes later I was leaning on the counter by the window and I had a great view of the street and the office across it. Next to me were five stools lined up for customers to sit and drink their coffee and eat their sandwiches and watch the world go by. But while the drugstore was quite busy, for some reason nobody much felt like sitting next to me. And that was just fine. My day had been too long already and I wasn't much in the mood for company.

I had bought a coffee and a sandwich. I couldn't resist, and I didn't want to take up space in the store without paying rental. The sandwich looked great but I left it untouched on the plate in front of me. The coffee I held cupped in one hand and then periodically in the other. I enjoyed the feeling of warmth that spread with ease through my well-conducting steel-titanium skin and I enjoyed the smell of the coffee as the steam wafted up into the chemical analyzer that sat in the middle of my face in a geometric approximation of a human nose.

I watched the office across the street, flipping through a

selection of optical filters to try to cut the glare and reflection from all that glass. That helped. I could see now that the desks inside the office were arranged in a kind of wide V, the point farthest away, to give all of the staff the benefit of the big windows. And while that meant the workers within could look right out, it also meant that people on the outside could look *in*, admiring the five men and two women as they worked and typed and smoked and drank coffee. One guy was even eating a sandwich, the green paper being unwrapped on his desk the same green paper that enclosed the sandwich on the counter in front of me.

As locations went, I could see why Emerson Ellis had picked it. The office was well placed on a good street with a lot of amenities within easy reach.

Emerson Ellis, it turned out, was some kind of real estate magnate, and already I didn't like him. I didn't like him because I was suspicious of alliterative names. I didn't know if that was some natural instinct or programming. Perhaps my creator, Professor Thornton, had once known a character with alliterative initials and they hadn't got on and I'd inherited that trait along with a lot more of old Thornton, rest his soul.

I also didn't like Emerson Ellis because he wasn't at the damn office. I knew he wouldn't be, but after following his echo all over two cities already today I wanted to come and make sure for myself. I felt a solenoid spark even as I thought about the target and his infuriating habit of not being where I wanted him to be.

Then I looked down at my unopened sandwich and I switched my coffee to my other hand and I felt a little better.

Emerson Ellis was the boss, and to remind everyone of that fact he had named his company after himself and he had put that name in large gold letters across the field of glass that formed the street-side wall of his office. Emerson Ellis Building and Construction. There was also a telephone number and an address, as if prospective clients staring up at the gold letters a foot high each couldn't remember where they were.

Inside the office window was an easel and on that easel was a large rectangular card, a yard wide and almost that high. On the card was an illustration of squares and rectangles that looked exactly like the kind of building development you wouldn't want to live next to. The easel and its card were angled in the window so people could stop and look and be suitably impressed, if not mildly disgusted. The card proudly boasted that it was a development worth ten million dollars and I was surprised they hadn't put a chaise lounge out on the sidewalk for people of a nervous disposition to faint onto.

Emerson Ellis had a nice thing going. Business was good. So good the boss apparently didn't have to do any actual work anymore. That was the kind of business you could aspire to. But some of us had to work for a living.

Robots included.

Today was no different. Today I had a job to do and it was a job for which Ada would collect a nice paycheck. Maybe not enough to build a concrete monstrosity like the one on display in the real estate office window, but you had to start somewhere.

Of course, if today had gone according to plan, Emerson Ellis wouldn't be building the development either. A lot of people were going to be disappointed but probably a lot more were going to be relieved. It wasn't often that my job intersected with a public service.

There was only one problem as I sat there at the drug store counter with a coffee that was cooling and a sandwich that was curling at the edges and that problem was Emerson Ellis himself and the fact that I couldn't find him to kill him.

In fact, nobody could find him, whether they wanted to turn off his lights or buy him a scotch.

That wasn't to say he was *missing*, as such. Far from it. It was just that he wasn't anywhere that people knew. Not his friends, not his coworkers. Emerson Ellis was a busy man. Emerson Ellis was a successful man. He didn't get where he was today by telling people where he was at any given moment.

I had hoped to get lucky, that luck helped to not a small degree by the fact that I was a private detective and that finding people was one of those things that private detectives were supposed to be good at.

Well, I *had* been a private detective. I was still programmed for it even if that wasn't my job anymore—not since Ada, a computer designed to make a profit, had discovered that killing people paid rather more than just finding them—and I was still registered and licensed and insured and listed in the Los Angeles telephone directory as such and we kept the office in the Cahuenga building and it still had THE ELECTROMATIC DETECTIVE AGENCY stenciled on the door, although in gold letters only one-sixth the size of the ones painted on the glass of Emerson Ellis Building and Construction.

As a cover, being a private eye was as good as any, if not better. As the last robot in the world, my existence wasn't a secret, but it wasn't advertised; if you knew about me or found out about me then you'd know I was a private eye and that was life as we know it.

But despite my new programming as an assassin, courtesy of Ada, I still had my old primary programming as a private eye from Professor Thornton. I may not have remembered what the weather was yesterday or who the president of the United States was at the moment but I sure as hell knew the criminal statutes of the state of California and I knew how to pick a lock and to listen to a conversation in a bar without getting caught doing it.

These skills were programmed in. Hardwired into my permanent store along with the flags of the world and the names of fifty-two different kinds of nautical knots and how to tie them. And while that meant I could probably do a passable job of sailing a ship, it also meant that while I was out doing my real job of killing people for money without getting caught I could also sneak around and be discrete and investigate that which needed investigating to make my real job not just easier but *possible*.

Because the first thing you had to do when you wanted to kill someone? You had to *find* them.

5

Since walking out of the office with Emerson Ellis's name and office address on that little strip of ticker tape, I'd spent most of that afternoon looking for him and here's what I found:

Nothing.

Emerson Ellis was successful. I had gotten that idea after just a few phone calls, the first step in my unsatisfying afternoon flitting between Los Angeles and Beverly Hills. I called his office five times with five different voice modulations from four different telephone booths dotted around Hollywood and downtown. Just being careful. I spoke to three different women, secretaries or typists or both, one of whom had developed the no doubt useful skill of being able to type while she handled telephone inquiries. I asked for the boss. I was a client late for a meeting. I was a potential client interested in the pile of concrete on display on the big card in the window. I was Emerson Ellis's dentist. I was calling from city hall about a permit and there was a problem with the paperwork and Emerson Ellis really had better call me back *tout de suite* or there was going to be a delay. An *expensive* delay.

There were no dice to be had. Emerson Ellis was busy and successful and he didn't need to tell his staff where he was and he didn't need to have his secretaries fill out his diary for the week. If he was on vacation, nobody knew it. If he was at the dentist, nobody questioned why his dentist was apparently calling to say he was late.

With no Emerson Ellis to investigate, I investigated Emerson Ellis Building and Construction. It was as successful and busy as its founder. It dealt with high-end commercial real estate, which meant several of the staff had big houses with swimming pools thanks to their sizeable commission earnings. The rest had anything from a quiet bungalow to a second-floor apartment. All of this thanks to the Los Angeles and Beverly Hills telephone directories and a nice woman called Cheryl at information who I spoke to for a good length of time. She had a pet corgi called Napoleon. Napoleon sounded like a nice dog and Cheryl sounded like a nice owner. When she asked what I did I told her I was in confidential inquiries. She seemed to like that, the way she laughed. And once she knew she was talking to a private eye she was keen to help, although she was equally keen to remind me that she really shouldn't be doing this and when she gave me Emerson Ellis's home telephone number and his home address she gave it in a whisper that must have sounded at least a little suspicious to the other directory-assistance girls sitting around her.

But it worked. I had Emerson Ellis's address—*addresses*, plural. Because Emerson Ellis was successful and what successful man didn't own five houses?

I still didn't know where Emerson Ellis was but I had a feeling in my logic gates that I was getting closer.

His telephone numbers were less useful. Five calls to his office was one thing. A call to each of his houses was another entirely. I didn't know who wanted him dead or why and nor did I care, but it occurred to me that Emerson Ellis might have been missing for a reason. Maybe with his success came a paranoia, or maybe he really did know that someone was out to get him. Calling his private numbers was out. If he was holed up at one of his homes I didn't want to give him any reason to be worried, at least more than he was already. I'd just have to go and visit him in person. But before that I parked myself outside his office in Beverly Hills with a sandwich and a coffee and watched a while, in case the boss came back, in case the boss really was there all along and just didn't want to be bothered. When you're the boss, you only take the calls you want to take, after all.

His office was buzzing like a beehive. People came and went. None of them was Emerson Ellis, and unless he had locked himself in the restroom, he really wasn't in.

I sat at the counter in the drugstore and watched the office for an hour. Then I checked my watch. Then I pulled the list of addresses Cheryl from information had given me up out of my memory and in front of my optics and I crosschecked them against the maps I pulled up out of my permanent store. I frowned, on the inside.

My coffee was cold. I unwrapped my sandwich. It was

two slices of rye bread and enough pastrami to pack into a mid-sized suitcase for a long vacation. It was a shame to waste it, but I couldn't eat it even if I wanted to.

Instead I stood up and left the sandwich and coffee where they were and I headed out into the street. There was a trash can right by the door on the inside of the drugstore but I couldn't bring myself to kill the sandwich or the coffee.

Emerson Ellis, however, was another matter.

6

Emerson Ellis owned five private properties. These included a city apartment that was more like the entire top floor of a building in West Hollywood, another smaller affair in downtown LA, and three houses, one in the Hollywood Hills near Griffith Park, one in Burbank near the giant lot of a movie studio, and one in Phoenix, Arizona.

The apartments were a bust. I got in easily, even to the big two-floor penthouse, on account of the fact that both premises were empty of anything except very expensive thin air. The concierges of both buildings were more than happy to let me take a look around. Both were impressed that a robot PI wanted their assistance, and I suspected both were a little disappointed by the empty rooms when they unlocked them for me. There were no dead bodies and no bloodstains and no bricks of dope in sight.

The two houses in Los Angeles were a different matter. I

headed to the one in Burbank first and when I arrived I thought I'd entered the movie studio back lot next door by accident. The house was a curious mix of Adobe and late classic Grecian, a rank of ionic columns holding up a terracotta roof and the whole thing wrapped in rough plaster. It didn't work in the slightest.

The building was new. So new that the columns, walls, and roof were all there was. The whole place was surrounded by chain-link fences, and there were the tools of construction all over the place and a big placard on the inside of the fence that proclaimed this monstrosity to be YET ANOTHER EMERSON ELLIS DEVELOPMENT.

So he was using his own company to build himself a new house. Good for him. If I owned a building company and wanted a house built then I'd call myself too.

But it was evident that he wasn't here. Nobody was. The place was locked up and the construction tools lay just where the laborers had left them whenever that had been.

That left the house around the back of Griffith Park. It was pushing six o'clock and traffic was going to be all kinds of hell but it wasn't like I had to stop for dinner.

The house in Griffith Park was infinitely more interesting if only for the fact that it was the only one out of the four properties I'd been to that day that was both complete and furnished and it looked like it had been that way for a good century or more.

The Griffith Park house was a gray shingle mansion that looked like it should have been balanced on a hilltop in New England instead of California. There were porticos and arched windows and a covered porch and a front door big enough to drive my car through if it wasn't at the summit of a face of stairs that looked like you needed oxygen and crampons to ascend. On the left side of the house was a big bay window through which I could see a lot of books in tall dark bookcases. On the right side the wall of the house was flatter but that flat wall just kept going up and up until it broke free of the main house and turned itself into a tower complete with a balcony a princess could lean on as she tried to catch sight of her forbidden lover on a moonlit night in Renaissance Italy. All of this was planted at the end of a driveway as long as the Pacific Coast Highway and twice as scenic. It was the kind of house you could go inside of and not come out until a half dozen presidents and their mistresses had filed through the Oval Office.

I had to admit I liked the thing and I stood there liking it quite a while after I'd pulled the car up in front. The sun was heading to bed and in the gathering gloom the house looked like another transplant from a studio back lot, like Emerson Ellis's Burbank property, only this one would be occupied by a pale gentleman with sharp fangs and a big black cape.

I thought twice about mounting the stairs but had come to a decision and was about to make an attempt on the north face when the front door opened and a man stepped across the threshold. He was wearing a gray pinstripe morning suit with crisp wing collars and a cravat you could go to sleep under. The posy pinned to his buttonhole was big enough to throw over your shoulder at a wedding.

He wasn't Emerson Ellis. He looked more likely to be the

butler and he looked like he'd been built with the house back in eighteen hundred and frozen stiff.

"Can I help you, sir?" he asked in a way that didn't require his mouth to move any.

I lifted my hat and held it there at altitude.

"I'm sorry to bother you," I said, "but I was wondering if the master of the house would be at home?"

The butler lifted his chin and pointed his nostrils at me. "I'm afraid Mr. Ellis is not at home to receive guests, but if you would leave your card I will ensure he contacts you at his earliest convenience."

I lowered my hat back onto my head. I stayed at the bottom of the stairs and the butler stayed at the top. Neither of us moved. I wondered if maybe he was a robot too.

"Mr. Ellis is not at home to receive guests, or is just plain not at home?"

The butler's lips twitched, which was a neat trick as they hadn't moved so far in our conversation.

"I am not at liberty to discuss the whereabouts of my employer, Mister . . . ?"

I reached into my pocket and pulled out a card. I wondered about folding it into a miniature paper airplane and launching it up to the butler but decided instead to walk up the steps and deliver it myself. The butler watched me hike up the stairs and then looked at me once I was at the top.

I offered the card from between two steel-titanium fingers and the butler did his best not to touch the card at all while taking it. I watched his eyes move over the text. The lip twitched again and this time it stayed twitched. This close I could see he didn't have any fangs, at least.

"As I said," said the butler, "I am not obliged to divulge the movements of Mr. Ellis to anyone."

"You don't need to tell me about his movements. I just want to know if he is currently stationary in the fourth drawing room on the left."

I was bluffing. I may have been a robot but I didn't have X-ray vision and while I could feel heat it wasn't like I could see the glowing outline of somebody through a wall. It occurred to me that both of these things would actually have been quite handy, times like this. Maybe I could ask Ada for an upgrade.

The butler gave me both barrels as he lifted his nose a little higher and set his sights on a far distant horizon. I wondered if that was where Emerson Ellis was.

"If you wish to talk to Mr. Ellis," said the butler, "I suggest you speak to his attorney. I would be quite happy to furnish you with the particulars."

I shrugged. "So his attorney knows where he is? He'd be the only one who does. Seems nobody in this town knows."

The butler stiffened the muscles in his already rock-solid neck. "Indeed," he said, not meaning anything at all except get the hell off of my lawn.

"In fact, I'm going to assume that Mr. Emerson Ellis is not at home and hasn't been for some time. Is that assumption anything close?"

That did it. The butler moved an eyebrow a half-inch upwards. I almost gave him a round of applause. The eyebrow stayed where it was while the eyeball underneath rolled down to look at the card I'd handed over.

"A private investigator?"

I nodded, just a little. "Confidential inquiries."

The butler nodded just a little himself. Then he pivoted on the heel of one polished black shoe like he was on hinges and he gestured with his arm.

"I think you had better come inside," he said, in case I hadn't got the picture.

I'd got it all right. I adjusted my hat and I went into the house.

7

The interior of Emerson Ellis's hillside hideaway appeared to be made entirely out of interlocking wooden panels all stained a uniformly dark brown. The hallway was bordered by a staircase on one side and on the other by a wall with a sideboard against it big enough to row across the Atlantic in. There was a chandelier above and a Persian carpet below and the former of these buzzed slightly.

I decided I didn't like the house. It looked like a New England mansion and it would have been better for all concerned if it moved back there at once. This was not a house for the California climate. It felt hot and stuffy in the evening and I imagined it would be worse during the day. With the butler sewn into his penguin suit I could picture him ending each and every day with an ice bath.

Right now the butler was looking at his feet. I followed his gaze. He'd put a lot of elbow grease into the shine on his shoes and I thought he wanted me to congratulate him when he spoke again without looking up.

"I suppose one can be trusted, in your line of work?"

Then he looked up. He'd begun to wring his hands in front of the middle button of his waistcoat.

I nodded. The butler was defrosting so I went right on in. "As I said, confidential inquiries are my specialty. I need to find your employer on a private matter. I tried his Beverly Hills office today but he failed to make an appearance, so I thought I'd try a personal visit to his other listed properties. I found two of these empty and one under construction. That only left one more in the state of California." I used my hat to point around the woodwork. "This house seems to be the only one that is actually a house."

The butler nodded. "Myself and Mrs. Hurst keep the house in good running order, sir."

Sir. As the butler continued to warm I found myself moving up in the world. Keep going and maybe I'd have a house and butler myself one day.

"Mrs. Hurst?"

"The, ah, wife, sir," said the butler, gesturing vaguely somewhere behind. "She is head house parlor maid for Mr. Ellis."

"You haven't seen him in a while, have you? Just like everyone else?" The butler nodded. Fine, sign language would do me. We could use semaphore if it would help and there was a flag at hand. I looked over the butler's shoulder. "Mrs. Hurst know any more?"

At this the butler shrugged and said, "She did see him last, but that was, oh, a week ago. She said that she heard him rummaging around upstairs, sir. She inquired if he required assistance and found him packing a case, and rather in a hurry he was too, sir. She said he didn't answer her and didn't say a thing at all, sir, but when she tried to help he shouted at her and flew out of the room, knocking her clean over. She said he was in quite a rage, sir."

The butler looked worried so I gave him my best encouraging smile, which was completely invisible, so instead I said:

"Go on."

"Well, sir," the butler went on. "She ran downstairs after him but, well, she's not as young as she once was. Too late she saw Mr. Ellis leaving in one of his cars. He hadn't even closed the front door after him."

"I see," I said.

"Mrs. Hurst was in quite a state, sir. I had to make two whole pots of tea just for her. And she used all the honey that was in the pantry."

I nodded. "Understandable," I said. "And quite sensible. You're a good man, Hurst."

The butler seemed pleased with this, as far as I could tell with a face that wouldn't crack.

"Any idea where he went?" I asked.

The butler shook his head and shrugged at the same time.

"There is one more property on my list. An address out in Phoenix, Arizona," I said. "Any chance he was heading out that way?"

"He has a house there, yes," said the butler. "It's possible that was his ultimate destination—in fact, I even telephoned ahead. Mr. Ellis has a . . . well, a business associate, I think you would call her, who lives in the city. One of his managers, I believe. A Ms. P. Garcia. Under normal circumstances we would call ahead and she would arrange to have the house ready for him. This time he had already left and we didn't know where he was going, but she said she would open the house and then call back."

"And she did?"

Hurst nodded. "The next day, at around ten o'clock. Mr. Ellis had failed to arrive."

"Okay. Which car did he take?"

"Ah, it was the Jaguar, sir. E-Type. An English import, like myself"—a smile and a chuckle here, me and the butler were practically war buddies now—"dark green, right-hand drive."

"Okay." That was something. "Can you get me the license plate?"

"Ah, yes, sir. If you will wait here, I can fetch the relevant documentation."

The butler gave me a slight bow and then he turned and vanished into the woodwork. He was gone a while and while he was gone I looked around and I turned my audio receivers up. There was no sound except for what I assumed was the butler looking through a file of paperwork in a study somewhere and the rattle of someone in the kitchen. Mrs. Hurst, probably.

I thought the butler was telling the truth. Nobody could be that rusty otherwise. His paycheck depended on his employer and his employer skipping town a week ago was clearly playing on the man's nerves.

Emerson Ellis hadn't gone to his house in Phoenix, but then with a car you could drive other places than Arizona. The problem here was that my jurisdiction, as far as a paid assassin can be said to have one, was southern California, and even then was mostly limited to Los Angeles and its neighbors. It was purely for practical reasons—I couldn't be out of range of my office, as I had to go back at least once a day to get the memory tape slowly turning in my chest swapped out for a fresh one and to get a top-up charge on my batteries. The batteries were okay. They could go for days, even weeks, before they were flat, but as my memory was the limiting factor, why risk it?

The butler came back in six minutes and twenty-two seconds and he handed me a yellow slip of paper. It was the title to a 1963 Jaguar E-type, British racing green, six-cylinder, 3.8 liters. It was a lot of car. It was a shame that Emerson Ellis was missing and Vaughan Delaney was dead because I thought they would have got along rather well.

"Thanks," I said. I took a picture of the title with the cameras in my eyes and then I took a second just to be sure. I handed the title back and the butler nodded and squeezed it gently with his hands. I headed for the door and he opened it for me. There was no ski lift at the top so I had to make the stairs on my own, and when I got to the bottom I turned around as the butler called down.

"I hope you find him, sir."

I lifted the hat from my head and gave it a little wave like a half-hearted revolutionary from a small Caribbean island.

I wanted to find him too, but I wasn't sure Mr. and Mrs. Hurst were going to be too pleased about what I planned to do with their employer when I did.

As I drove off up the driveway I looked in the rearview mirror. The butler was still standing where he was and now he was joined by a woman of the same age wearing a black dress and a white apron and small hat in the same colors.

Of course, once I'd found Mr. Emerson Ellis I'd have to come back to the big gray house and have another chat with the Hursts. When their boss disappeared for a second time in a permanent fashion the police would come a-knocking and the two servants would remember a big robot who came one early evening and asked a lot of questions.

One thing about this business was that leaving such loose ends untied was a *very* bad idea indeed.

8

I woke up in the computer room that sat out back of the office of the Electromatic Detective Agency. It was six in the morning and already the sun was rising high and casting a deep shadow over the brown brick of the building across the street, the building that was the first thing I saw each and every morning I woke up in the alcove in the computer room.

I never remembered this, of course, but I knew it to be true.

Around me Ada's lights flashed and her dials spun and several miles of magnetic data tape flew in one direction or another between big reels on the big computer mainframes.

I reached up and unplugged myself. The cable was fat and gray and made of a soft, corrugated plastic. The port was in my chest behind a hatch and as I closed that hatch I noticed it was a different color than the rest of me and that it arched outwards a little, like it was shaped to fit something larger than what was currently behind it, which was my memory—an ingenious piece of micro-engineering that allowed two reels of magnetic tape to be shrunk down and packed into my chest. I had a fresh reel in there right now.

That Professor Thornton had been a clever guy.

Ada hadn't spoken. I stepped out of the alcove and I did up my shirt. It seemed a little tighter across the chest thanks to the curved plate but the buttons stayed where I put them well enough.

There was a small table in the computer room and a single chair and on the back of my chair was my jacket. On the table was the early edition of today's newspaper, and on the newspaper was my hat and a paperback book.

I slipped the jacket off the chair and slipped it onto my back. I picked the hat up and put it on the ear of the chair and then I looked at the newspaper and moved it a little on the table.

My attention was really on the paperback book. There was a man and a woman on the front and the pair was running from a tentacled monster. The woman didn't look too happy about it but that might have been more to do with the fact that she was wearing nothing but a chain-mail bikini while her hero wore a tinfoil overall and a fishbowl over his head.

I opened the book and found several pages with bent-over corners. Someone had been reading. Maybe it had been me.

"Any good, Ray?"

I looked up into the corner of the room.

"Hard to tell," I said, "on account of the fact that I can't remember a thing about it."

Ada laughed and then she stopped laughing and all I could hear were the tapes rolling and the click of the clock above the door that led out into the main office.

I went over to that door and I opened it. The office beyond was quiet. There was a big window behind the desk and the sun was coming in through the half-closed slats. I counted the motes of dust dancing in the sunbeams. When I got to eleven thousand two hundred I got bored and I turned back around.

"Anything on the list for today, Ada?"

A light flashed. "Working on it, Ray."

I nodded. Okay.

"Any pickups?"

Pickups were jobs that were ongoing, and they needed picking up as I couldn't remember what had happened yesterday. It was all recorded on my memory tape, sure, but yesterday's memory tape was sitting in the storage room that was accessed from a secret door on the other side of the office.

The advantage to this short-term memory was that I was pretty safe. If I ever got caught, or fell into the wrong hands, nobody would learn anything because I didn't know anything. What I did know was that I was a robot assassin but I had no idea how many people I'd killed for greenbacks, or even if I had killed anyone at all.

But Ada knew. She was a computer the size of a room. She remembered everything.

So a pickup meant her briefing me on the current caseload and the latest developments, and she did that by getting me to plug back in so she could roll through the edited highlights of the relevant memory tapes I brought back in each day. On the face of it this system sounded awkward, and I'm sure it would be were it not for the fact that two computers can talk to each other pretty fast.

The clock above the door clicked on toward seven a.m. I pursed my lips, or I pretended to, and I decided I liked that expression. It seemed to help me think.

"Ah . . . Ada?"

"A gal can only collate so much data at once, chief."

I shrugged. "Okay," I said, and then I went to the table. I picked up the paperback and opened it to page one. It occurred to me I could have been working on this book for months, or forever.

I sat in the chair and I began to read. Two minutes later I put the paperback down when Ada spoke. Our plucky hero and his naked companion had already survived an asteroid storm and a solar flare and now their ship was being boarded by pirates from K19 and I hadn't even had any breakfast yet.

"Okay, chief," said Ada. "We have one open case and one new job. No need to buckle yourself in, kid. The pickup is easy as the job is temporarily on hold."

"Okay." I stayed sitting down.

"The pickup: one Emerson Ellis, real estate magnate. No timeline on this one, which is just as well as you haven't found him yet. You've spent a day on his tail and we know he's probably not in Los Angeles anymore. He might be in Phoenix. You have his photograph and the address of his business and several properties he owns around the city. You also have a telephone number for Phoenix to call for an update."

I nodded. Phoenix could be a problem. Even if I could've

flown out and back in a day, there was an associated risk with me being out of range of the office. If everything went smoothly, I'd be there and back and happily in my alcove. If there was even one flight delay, I could spend the rest of eternity rusting in the desert air after my memory tape hit the end of the reel, an event I wasn't sure I wanted to experience and which didn't sound like it would do me any good at all. And that was if I was even able to get on an airplane in the first place. I might not have had any luggage to check, but I weighed half a ton on my own and that sounded more than a little problematic.

And all that without knowing whether the target was in Phoenix in the first place.

I nodded again and I said, "Okay, got it. Lucky that job is open-ended. We'll just sit and wait."

"Right, chief. We just need to keep an ear to the ground for when Mr. Ellis gets back to LA—if he ever left it—and then you can take him out for a quiet drink, whether he wants to or not. But it's back-burner stuff for now. We've got a new job in and boy-howdy is this a doozy."

I got comfortable. Ada's tapes spun and the lights flashed and she told me all about it.

She was right. It was a doozy.

When Ada was done I whistled. It came out pretty good, less like a boiling kettle than I had anticipated. When I was done Ada laughed and I swore she finished by taking a drag on her fourth cigarette of the morning.

The clock above the door clicked over. Seven in the morning. The day was young and the job was hot but I didn't move from the table. Ada smoked in my mind and I thought I'd like to get a cup of coffee. I wondered if I always felt like a cup of coffee after Ada laid out a brief. I don't know. I didn't remember.

I watched the clock. It clicked over two more minutes and then the tapes on the computer bank to my left came to a halt and then reversed direction.

Ada was thinking.

"You don't like it?" she asked.

I frowned on the inside.

"It's not my favorite."

"How would you know that, Raymondo? You don't remember any other jobs."

"That may be true, Ada," I said, "but right about now I feel more like taking my chances in Phoenix, Arizona."

"I get it," Ada said, "but airfares are a killer. A guy your size we'd need to book two seats there and back and even then might need to give the plane a push-start."

I looked up into the corner. I was pretty sure Ada was looking at me over the rim of a cup of steaming black coffee and I thought again how I'd love a cup even though I couldn't drink the stuff and then the feeling and the image both were gone and I was back in the computer room.

"Are you sure it'll work?" I asked.

"Sure, why not," said Ada. She sounded as convinced as I felt and not any more.

"Eight o'clock tonight?"

"On the dot, chief."

"Okay." I looked at the clock. It was seven-oh-seven in the morning. I had twelve hours and fifty-three minutes until the curtain rose. I just wasn't sure I wanted to see the show.

"You got a plan, Ray?"

I shrugged. I put my hat on and from the back of the

door I lifted my trench coat. I slipped it on and did it up and the top button felt tight. So tight it slid out of its hole the first time but it stayed put the second.

I wanted to ask Ada about my new chest piece but the new job was doing a number on my transistors. I wanted that to be done before anything else. I only hoped I could remember to ask the boss about my repairs later.

"I'll go check out the location, make sure I know what's what. Last thing anyone wants—the client included—is for this to go wrong, right?"

"On the money, chief. Reconnaissance. I like it. You'd make a great detective."

I *hrmmed*. It sounded like a chainsaw in need of a good oil.

"First I have to make a phone call," I said. Then I opened the door and I headed into the main office.

I closed the door behind me. Then I stood in the office by the door and I thought about the new job.

It was a little unusual. It was difficult. It was also potentially dangerous. I hoped Ada had negotiated a good fee.

I shrugged and adjusted my hat and reached for the telephone on the big desk by the window.

9

It was heading toward midmorning by the time I pulled up outside the Bacchanalian, which was by all accounts one of the best Italian restaurants in Hollywood and so named because it only served certain hand-picked wines that were imported from the home country and cost the same as my Buick per bottle, if not per glass.

I sat in the car and I looked at the front of the place and figured there was some inverse correlation between how good a joint was and the amount of signage on display, which in this case was virtually nonexistent. If you had to ask what the restaurant was called then you couldn't afford a plate of their spaghetti, let alone a drop of their *vini*.

The telephone call to Phoenix had been a bust. I didn't know who I was calling but the name on the computer printout that was sitting on the blotter on the big desk said P. GARCIA, and when I rang the number a woman answered and said that no, he hadn't shown. I said thanks and she hung up and didn't even say good-bye. Maybe that was how they did things in Phoenix, Arizona.

After the call I went down to the garage and I got the car out and I headed to the address provided by our new client. I didn't know who they were and that was none of my business. I didn't know why they wanted the target dead, although in this instance I could guess. That wasn't any of my business either.

But it didn't mean I wasn't interested.

The amount of information we got with each job varied. We got a name, usually an occupation. Most times we got a photograph but sometimes we didn't and instead the client had arranged a finger man to come point the target out. Being a finger man seemed like a risky job on account of the fact that it was their name that was usually next on the job sheet.

What we never got were *reasons*. We were paid what we were paid to do the thing and to not ask questions. Business was business and a job was a job and, as Ada might have said, money makes the world go around.

For this job, we had more than a name and a photo. The client had given us these details and more besides. We not only knew who the target was but we knew all about him and that included knowing where he liked to eat.

But there was more.

The client had given us a whole entire *plan*, a plan which led me to the Bacchanalian, a little Italian restaurant hidden in a quiet street like a secret whispered to a lover. A restaurant where the target would be enjoying his weekly dinner outing in just a little over ten hours.

The target's name was Zeus Falzarano, and he was a

gangster. It was my job to kill him.

Except in order to kill him, I had to do something else first.

I had to save his life.

Zeus Falzarano was a real piece of work. He was Italian, although nobody who ever called him that survived long enough to apologize, on account of the fact that he was born on the island of Sicily, which, at least according to Falzarano, was as Italian as President Kennedy's maiden aunt.

Sources said Zeus Falzarano was seventy-nine years old but didn't look a day over sixty-seven. He was born in a town called Medina and he didn't leave it until he was somewhere in his mid-fifties. The story went that he was a patriotic man and one fiercely proud of his home town, and saw no reason to leave it until the Italian police, who, unlike Falzarano, considered Sicily to be well within their jurisdiction, moved in to dethrone him. Because Falzarano loved his town and his island so much he spent the first fifty-five years of his life slowly taking the place over.

He was an astute businessman. The sources said it was a gift, like a savant who can compose an opera without ever hearing a violin or paint the skyline of Paris without having ever seen it and maybe that source was getting a little poetical, but I got the point. Falzarano had built himself up and he built an empire with it, a family-run business that involved large amounts of money that was mostly attached to guns, girls, drugs, gambling, and investment in local infrastructure, construction, and business, and that mostly went unreported to the authorities. With all this money he paid people he could and he made those he couldn't pay disappear. Over the course of three decades he owned not only his precious town of Medina but most of the island of Sicily and a good chunk of the Italian mainland and bits of Europe as well as a lot of the criminal trade that ran east to west from Russia to France.

So he was gifted. Born to it. He was a criminal mastermind and he was apparently a real swell guy to work for and people liked him a lot.

Sure. Put a gun to their head and I figure most people will like a lot of things if you ask them politely.

The story was that when the Italian *polizia* got sick of Zeus Falzarano running the courts and the judges and maybe even the president and quite possibly the Pope, he moved out of Medina and emigrated to the one country where he could really work on his spirit of free enterprise.

The United States of America.

Why he chose Los Angeles was anyone's guess, but once he got here he bought a great big house that looked like a castle that was buried in a valley in the Hollywood Hills and he set up this new arm of his little family business.

He fit right in. He bought up local crime syndicates. He bought up local police. Those who couldn't be bought he tried to eliminate, but American crime was of a different flavor than the sort he was used to and the gang wars that followed were long and bloody for folk on both sides of the law and Falzarano fared badly. Badly enough to lock himself away in his house and never come out. A lot of people didn't like him and more than a few of those people wanted to send his body floating back across the Atlantic.

So, just like any other Hollywood mogul, then.

What Falzarano did up in his house once the dust had settled was anyone's guess. He was old and getting older. Nobody had seen him for a couple of years, only his boys, his inner circle imported from Sicily along with their suits and their cars and their aftershave.

There was a rumor he'd taken up a hobby in his enforced retirement. Motion pictures. Sources said he bought into a movie studio called Playback Pictures and Playback Pictures did pretty well until the head producer, a guy called Chip Rockwell, had an accident of the fatal variety.

According to Ada, I knew a thing or two about Chip Rockwell. I believed her, but of course I couldn't remember anything and all my circuits told me I didn't know the guy from Adam.

After the death of Chip Rockwell, Playback Pictures wasn't the same. Maybe Falzarano had gotten bored of it because soon after he turned his hand to another hobby. This one was book writing and the magnum opus that came out of it was called *I Didn't Have Chip Rockwell Killed But If I Did Here's How I Would Have Done It.*

I asked Ada about that. She said it was a laugh riot. She also said it was a bestseller and that there had been a court case over it that hadn't done the sales any harm at all. Quite the opposite in fact.

There was another story that said Zeus Falzarano had bought all the copies of the book himself, but that was just a story.

Then something interesting happened. Falzarano ventured out of his castle with a couple of Sicily's finest gangland exports glued to his side. He turned up at a nightclub and so did half the hoods of Los Angeles and

KILLING IS MY BUSINESS

even a few from farther afield. That was news enough, at
least on the underground grapevine. What else was news
was the disappearance of a mobster called Bob Robertson,
a goon from New York employed by an East Coast kingpin
called Tieri. Maybe Falzarano had something to do with
that and maybe that was the reason that after the night on
the tiles he went back up to his house and never came
down again. That, or maybe the fact that the body of one of
Falzarano's boys was found dumped in the LA River
somewhere out in Compton a couple of days later.

Whatever the case, something had got Zeus Falzarano
scared again. The Los Angeles underworld was braced for
another gang war and Falzarano locked himself back up in
his castle. Word was that he was a target. Someone had put
a price on his head and that someone was probably Tieri.

Which is where I came in. I didn't know who the client
was and I didn't care, but someone had put a down payment
on Falzarano's life and it was my job to make sure we got
the rest of the money in good time.

The problem was that Falzarano was locked away in his
house in the hills again and sources reported he had
enough men and guns to extend the southern border of
California well into Mexico if he so desired. Getting to
Falzarano posed something of a conundrum.

Which is why our anonymous client had given us a
plan. They would start things off and then I would finish
things and everyone would be happy with one less
mafioso in Hollywood.

The secret to getting to Falzarano was getting into his
house—and Falzarano himself would provide the key.

The plan to get the key was, as Ada had said, a real doozy,

and was the reason I found myself casing out an Italian restaurant in Hollywood on a Wednesday morning and wondering what I had done with my life to get involved in a scheme like this.

The plan was simple. The client had laid the whole thing out. That didn't mean I had to like it, but it went like this:

Falzarano kept himself locked in his castle except for once-weekly excursions to his favorite restaurant. Call it an extravagance. Call it a flaw. But it was the best restaurant in town and that's what he did. He took an army with him and he came in through the back and he was as safe in the restaurant as he was in his own dining room.

Or so he thought.

Tonight at eight o'clock Falzarano and the boys would be enjoying their Chianti and linguine and talking about good times in the old country and someone was going to come and interrupt their dinner with a little light machine-gunning. Sure, Falzarano brought a lot of men with him, but all you had to do to get past them was bring more bullets.

It was going to be a massacre and the Bacchanalian wouldn't be open for business for quite a while. Falzarano, on the other hand, was going to be just fine, because I was going to be there to save his life.

This is where things got a little twisted. I asked Ada why Falzarano didn't just die in the restaurant along with the rest of his boys, and the answer was one I didn't like, along with the rest of all this.

Falzarano had to survive, because I was going to kill him *later*. I was going to use the restaurant attack to get into Falzarano's employ, and then all I had to do was hang around and wait for the word and then I'd get to work. The call in question might come tomorrow. It might come at Christmas. It didn't matter, because when it came I'd be at Falzarano's elbow and I'd be able to do the thing and then get out and the client would be so happy they'd insist on making a sizeable voluntary donation to a numbered bank account somewhere in a country that didn't ask a lot of questions.

And while I was catering to Falzarano's every whim just like the rest of his hoods, I'd have the opportunity to look around his house and put my metal nose into his business. The client, whoever they were, wanted to know what Falzarano was up to. Why, I didn't know, considering they were just going to send up the flag when it was time to remove Falzarano from the equation anyway. What did it matter if he spent his days in the house knitting sweaters?

That, however, was not my business. Killing was my business and it was a business I was good at so all I had to do was stop and wait and watch and have a look around and then when Venus was in conjunction with Mars and a black crow crowed three times on a red sky morning or whatever, I could get to the real work. This is what I did for money and, as Ada was fond of reminding me, a robot has to earn a living somehow.

I looked at the Bacchanalian and I shook my head and then I drove around the corner and parked under a tree where the shade was nice and the street was quiet and I reached over to the paperback book on the passenger side.

I started reading and I tried not to worry too much about what would happen if it all went wrong at eight o'clock tonight.

There was a lot riding on the fact that I was supposed to keep Zeus Falzarano alive.

10

At seven thirty that night I sat at my table in the Bacchanalian. Falzarano's entourage had the place to themselves but they didn't book the whole joint out; it was more that other customers were quietly discouraged at the door by the maître d'. The fact that he made no such attempt when I made my entrance suggested that he either liked the idea of a robot eating a fancy dinner at his restaurant or that he knew who I was and what I was doing here.

The inside of the place was quite nice. The doorway was a squeeze for a robot of my proportions and once inside I could see the joint was pretty tight in a way that most customers would call cozy. Personally I would have preferred a little more elbow room but I knew the place was due for redecoration in a little under a half hour anyway.

The front part of the restaurant was narrow and there were four tables lined up in a row running from the front to the rear. Once you hit the fifth table, the place opened out at the back with enough room for three tables abreast in four neat rows that kept going back until they hit the door for the kitchen and the restrooms and a small bar that was more for show than for sitting at.

As I'd seen from the outside, the front wall of the restaurant facing the sidewalk was made up of little rectangles of imperfect glass set into a lattice of wood that was painted black and that bulged out in the middle. The amount of wood and the bubbles in the glass made it hard to see out and hard to see in. Maybe that was the point. There was more of this Olde Worlde charm on the inside, where the black painted wood crawled over the walls and the low ceiling. Maybe this was what restaurants in Sicily looked like. I had no idea. All I knew was that Zeus Falzarano's favorite table was the one in the window.

At seven forty the place was full with Falzarano's boys sucking down spaghetti like it was rationed up at the big house and sucking down fine Italian wines in shades of red from thick crystal glasses that glittered and glowed in the candlelight. The candlelight did nice things to the front windows too, the imperfections catching the moving light and shining it back into the room. The place was cozy when it was empty and when it was full it was hot and loud. There was hardly enough room for the waiters to dance around the tables but they did it all the same.

And while there must have been thirty people enjoying themselves inside there were at least that many stationed outside on the sidewalk and across the street and down on every corner in a two-block radius. I'd watched them set themselves up earlier, a troop of dark men with dark hair and wearing dark suits leaning against lamp posts and storefronts and not doing anything except watching and smoking and feeling the weight of the guns they had hidden inside their expensive tailored jackets.

Once everyone was in place outside, the others had filed in from the back, through the kitchen, and Falzarano had headed straight for the table at the window. Two of his men went with him. I don't know how he picked them. Maybe there was a roster. It seemed like a good position to be in. You got to eat the finest Italian food in the city and whisper sweet nothings to the big boss about what a great job he was doing these days and how his taste in wine was truly excellent.

I was at the fourth table from the front, the last one before the restaurant widened out. The staff had been very accommodating, the maître d' even sending one of his white-jacketed minions to fetch the big carver chair from the back so I had something a little sturdier to sit on. It creaked underneath me but it would do. I sat facing the front. Before me was a table with two of Falzarano's boys, then an empty table formed some kind of buffer zone, and then there was the table in the window. Falzarano sat on my right, his back to the wall of the restaurant. One of his boys sat opposite the boss, the other sat with his back to the front windows.

I played with a breadstick or two and I ordered a bottle of something nice and as the sommelier fussed over it next to me I watched the man I was here to save.

Zeus Falzarano lived up to his name. I agreed with the sources who said he looked younger than he was. He was a big man. He sat at the table with his stomach pushed against it and the third of his double chins sagging over the collar of his shirt. He had a thin gray moustache and the hair on his head was thin too, but he'd brushed it sideways and plastered it down with something and I had to admit it didn't look too bad considering what he had to work with. He had a big hooked nose and eyebrows like tropical caterpillars and when he laughed, which was often, I saw he still had all of his teeth.

He looked like a mobster and he looked like he was proud of it. The two boys with him were tall and dark and handsome and they were clearly aficionados of their boss's hair cream, the way they'd sculpted their own coiffures, shining like wet plastic in the candlelight. The boys wore dark suits that were exquisitely tailored around the shoulders and they laughed and drank and ate with their boss. I turned up my audio receptors but heard nothing except the fussing of the sommelier at my left elbow. He was telling me all about the history of the region of the wine he had brought to show me and I just nodded and let him keep going. He had a nice warm accent and he burbled in a pleasing, discreet way.

Then he stopped. I looked up at him and he was holding the bottle in the crook of his arm and waved it near me like a young father showing off his newborn son and heir.

"Do you wish to . . . ah, taste the wine, *signore*?"

The sommelier was a young man with long hair that very nearly but not quite touched his collar. He seemed good at his job, although I wasn't the best judge of that, and he looked eager to please although there was an expression floating over his face like he was trying to remember if he'd left the gas on back in Florence.

I gave him my best smile but I'm not sure he saw it, so I just said, "I'm sure that'll be fine," and I let him get on with extracting the cork and letting the wine flow and I went back to watching Falzarano.

It was now seven fifty-two.

Eight minutes.

Falzarano and his boys were enjoying their party. I watched them drink and smoke and talk and not really do much eating.

Seven fifty-five.

I stood up. I had to push my table a little to make room and the legs squealed against the floor but nobody heard. The restaurant was busy and noisy and by now any passing interest in a robot like me having a nice Italian meal had evaporated.

I waited for a waiter to get out of the way and then I slid down the aisle until I was at the front of the restaurant. As I passed the third table from the front the two hoods there suddenly got very interested in me. They didn't get up but they stopped talking and stopped drinking and their eyes were on me all the time and each of them had a hand reaching inside a jacket pocket.

I reached Falzarano's table. The two boys sitting with their boss looked up at me and kept drinking with a feigned disinterest. The old man was talking and he didn't stop. Nor did he look at me. He was busy telling his boys a story and nothing was going to interrupt that.

Seven fifty-seven.

Falzarano's story finished when he took a mouthful of wine and when he was done swallowing he held the glass up to the candlelight and swirled the red liquid within and then he put the glass down. Then he looked at me with lips squeezed together like the wine had been lemon juice and not a Chianti that cost a hundred bucks a cup.

"I know you?" asked Falzarano. His voice was deep and rich and he had an accent to match. He asked the question in a way that suggested he wasn't interested in my answer. Then he lifted his glass and took a sip and while his face was buried in the glass I saw him look at me with eyes that were a bit wider than they had been before.

Seven fifty-eight.

His two boys took this as their cue, which was fine by me, because I was going to need a little room in exactly two minutes. The hood with his back to the window stood first. He buttoned the front of his jacket and then he held his hands politely crossed in front of his middle like he was the best man at a wedding. His friend on the end of the table stood as well, but this guy used one hand to pull back his jacket and the other to retrieve a nine-millimeter cannon which he pointed in my direction.

Seven fifty-nine.

I kept my optics on the boss and I gave him a little bow. Falzarano's eyes glittered as he gave the top of my head a once-over. That was fine. I was a robot. Oftentimes people's eyes glittered when they got close to me, like I was some kind of celebrity.

"Mr. Falzarano, it's a real pleasure," I said.

Falzarano cocked his head and then he picked up his napkin. He unfolded it and took some time doing it, and then he dabbed at the corners of his mouth like a man with nothing better to do. Then his head went over in the opposite angle like a dog listening for his master and then he opened his mouth to say something else.

If he said anything, I didn't hear what it was. Because as he opened his mouth the clock struck eight and then the shooting started.

11

That Olde Worlde frontage of the Bacchanalian restaurant exploded in a shower of thick glass shards and splintered black wood and from beyond the ruined portal came the fast snare-drum rattle of a machine gun. More than one, in fact, and possibly more than two as well.

Falzarano's boy at the front went down first, collapsing forward under the weight of the exploding window frame and the hail of high-caliber bullets. The table buckled under him but stayed upright. The bullets had torn through the man's upper torso and had kept going, ripping up his pal opposite who was thrown backward like he'd been tackled by line defense, the black nine millimeter that had been in his hand now spinning uselessly in the air. He fell onto the table behind him but there was nobody to catch him, as the two hoods sitting there were now missing their heads after the broadside caught them side-on. Their bodies sat jerking in their chairs as the fusillade began to disassemble the corpses with appreciable violence.

I assumed people were shouting but it was impossible to hear over the machine guns, even with my systems. The air was thick with flying lead and dust and smoke and glass and wood as the men out on the sidewalk raked the restaurant with gunfire, reducing tables and chairs and silverware and waiters and Falzarano's boys alike to so much particulate matter.

The barrage didn't seem to be letting up even though everyone was surely dead by now.

Except for Zeus Falzarano. He was safe and sound and protected by six feet ten inches of steel-titanium alloy. The wall against which he had been settled was recessed a little, which gave him a microscopic amount of cover from the front windows. That let him survive the initial tornado of debris after the shooters had opened up but in the chaos he ducked forward and down, which put him square in the way.

That was okay. It brought him closer to me and that was just where I needed him.

As the bullets came in through the gaping void where the fancy front windows had been, I stepped into the firing line and pushed the table and the dead guy slumped over it out of the way. Then I grabbed Falzarano and shoved him in front of me. I wrapped two arms around him and squeezed his bulk in. He seemed to get the picture and he kept his head low.

My chassis was between him and the shooters and the shooters didn't stop—in fact, they even shot a little harder, aiming squarely at me instead of panning back and forth like an office fan on a hot afternoon. Among the smoke now flew big orange sparks, around me and the man I was protecting. They lit up the smoke like flares and they fizzed and glowed like someone had set off a whole bunch of fireworks inside the wreckage of what had once been the best Italian restaurant in town.

I could feel it too. The bullets came hot and fast and they ricocheted off my back and into what was left of the walls and the ceiling and they peppered the floor and I'm sure a whole lot went right back out the maw and into the street. My suit was history. My skin was fine. I was made of an alloy that people at the Pentagon kept inch-thick files on and that the boys at NASA really wanted a closer look at. I'd need a buff and polish but I'd be fine so long as the punishment didn't last too much longer. The shooters on the sidewalk would run out of ammunition soon enough.

Whether they did or whether they figured their job was done, the bullets stopped coming in a single instant like someone had shut off a tap and the next thing I heard among the crackle of flames and the tinkle of falling glass was the slamming of a car door, once, twice, three times, and then that same car laying down rubber and blasting off down the street at a rate of knots.

And then it was quiet.

I stood up and loosened my grip on Zeus Falzarano. He was still breathing. I straightened up and he did too. He looked around the empty space in front of him that had once been a restaurant and was now a tangle of bodies and body parts and kindling, all salted generously with crumbled glass fragments.

Then he turned around and looked up at me. He still

had the napkin in his hand and with a dazed look he drew it up to his mouth and dabbed the corners again. He had a gash on his forehead that was leaking and the blood was pooling in his impressive eyebrows. He kept dabbing at the corners of his mouth before he realized he was bleeding and then he gasped and he applied the napkin to the cut.

I turned around, pushing debris out of my way with my feet. There were people outside on the street. Now that the shooters and their getaway car had gotten away some other cars had stopped in the middle of the road, their drivers and passengers half-out, balanced on running boards and hanging on doors as they stared open-mouthed at the scene before them. There were people on the sidewalk too, on both sides of the streets, looking and pointing and waving at others but all the while keeping the space in front of the restaurant clear, maybe wary of a gas leak or fire or something equally dangerous.

I didn't blame them. It looked like a bomb had gone off.

Among the crowd were the rest of Falzarano's entourage, who had peeled out of their alcoves and shadows and street corners and had come running, but only after the shooting had stopped, and not to save their boss but to check on whether they needed to find new employment in the morning. I figured that would probably be the case regardless of whether their boss was alive or dead—either their paychecks just got stopped rather suddenly, or Falzarano was going to be furious they spectacularly failed to stop the attack and would fire them anyway. But for the moment, the men just stood and stared at the smoking crater that had been the restaurant and then they looked at each other and they started shouting and shoving at the crowd to get them out of the way.

Then came the metallic rattle of car-mounted bells and flashing lights and from both ends of the street the sound of cars and trucks coming. Police, fire, ambulance, the works, roaring to the scene, converging on what was clearly the start of World War Three.

The lights and the bells seemed to snap Falzarano out of his daze. He looked around the wreckage, his eyes moving from one body to the next to the next, the realization that a sizeable chunk of his staff were dead slowly dawning.

He looked up at me with his rheumy old-man eyes and his jaw hanging a little slack. Then that jaw snapped shut and the eyes narrowed.

"Get me out of here," he said.

"Follow me," said I.

12

I took Zeus Falzarano through the back of the restaurant, pushing rubble aside as I led the way. I stepped over bodies and Falzarano did the same.

I was parked out back. I showed him to my car and even held the door open for him. Then I got in and I drove away from the restaurant and the lights and the sirens and the gathered crowds.

I drove and Falzarano held the napkin to his forehead with one hand and with the other he pointed, giving me directions with stabs of his index finger. This way. That way. Take a left. Right. Left. Never a street name, never a place. After a while he said, "Head north and keep going," so I did what he said and we drove in the Hollywood night, the robot and the mafioso.

Falzarano fell silent. I kept on driving. As I drove I thought that the plan was working, although I hadn't expected that level of carnage at the restaurant. The attack had been overkill but it had sure got Falzarano's attention, which was exactly the plan. Scare the old man back to his castle in the hills, only now with me at his side.

So far, so good.

We drove another half hour. The lights of the city vanished as we cut into the inky darkness of the hills. Falzarano kept his eyes on the road. Then he reached out and jerked his hand and I slowed and took a left.

There was a big gate in the way. It was a towering thing, arched and elaborate like the gates on an old cemetery. There were two big stone lions on either side, their claws raised and jaws agape but their anger frozen. They had no idea what was going on.

As we came up the car's headlights swept over two men in suits and hats who had emerged from the darkness and were jogging toward us on the other side of the gate. They were carrying rifles in their hands and they slowed and bent down and shielded their faces from the lights as they peered into the car.

Then they saw their boss sitting there with a bloody forehead and an angry look and they both jerked like they'd touched a live wire. One of them waved furiously at the other, like they weren't two feet apart. The other guy got the message well enough. He slung the strap of his rifle over his shoulder and got to work on the gate's giant lock.

The gate swung open and I pushed the accelerator. The Buick cruised down the sloping driveway. It took a full minute to get to the end, where the driveway looped around a fountain that stood in front of a big stone house. I brought the car to a rest and tried very hard to raise an eyebrow as I looked up out of the windshield.

To say the house was big was to say the Mona Lisa was a cute little sketch. I knew the place as Falzarano's castle and that was closer to the truth than I had expected. The whole thing was assembled from great gray stone blocks, their edges mathematically true but their faces rough. At each corner was a big square tower with windows and the windows had balconies. The tops of the towers were castellated but then so was the rest of the house, and behind those jigsaw teeth stood more men with rifles. I was almost disappointed they weren't armed with longbows.

The European Gothic effect was spoiled a little by the palm trees that lined the driveway and the big flowering plants that crowded around the castle. It was as though Count Dracula had uprooted and moved to the Bahamas and taken the best of Transylvania with him.

The fountain was big and it was in full swing, the water shooting up ten feet at the very least before turning around and heading back to Earth. When I turned the car off the sound of the fountain and the sound of crickets mixed in a pleasing way in the evening air.

Then came the sounds of feet running fast on gravel and of doors opening and closing. Next to me Falzarano was busy examining his bloody napkin.

Within a moment or two there were four people standing outside the car, leaning in to look, waving at each other with the big rifles they all seemed to carry. Everyone wore a suit and everyone wore a hat and they all had sunglasses on despite the hour. They weren't as pretty as the Beefeaters at the Tower of London but I'm sure they would have been just as good at guarding the crown jewels. On the other hand, his boys keeping watch down at the Bacchanalian had been the next thing to useless, apparently overlooking the obvious possibility of a drive-by assassination attempt.

Or maybe it was just obvious in retrospect. Or maybe they were in on it.

Falzarano hissed something in a language I wasn't programmed with and he unwound his window. He leaned out and waved the napkin like a bloodstained flag. He spoke fast and his men sprang into life, running around doing whatever men with high-powered rifles did when their boss was in a bad mood. Securing the perimeter, manning the lookouts, dusting off the rack, and boiling cauldrons of oil, etc.

Then Falzarano turned and waved the napkin at me and he pointed through the windshield.

There was a big garage set just off to the side of the castle and I could see it was attached to the main building. The garage was low and about as wide as a football field and had no fewer than four separate green double roller doors. As Falzarano shook his pointing finger in its direction the second door along folded up, more men on the inside silhouetted against the light as they pushed it up over their heads.

The inside of the garage was white and bright and there was an empty space next to a car that looked pretty sporty.

I got the drift. I put the Buick in gear and rolled her into the space. I stopped and looked at the car next to me. It was a Jaguar, in dark green. It was long and low and it crouched like its namesake, ready to pounce. The steering wheel was on the wrong side. An import from England.

There were other cars in the long garage. Two were

parked on the left of my Buick and after the Jaguar were four more. All of them shone in the bright garage lights.

I turned to Falzarano to apologize for not getting a scrub and wax before I parked my own car in his fancy garage but he was already heaving himself out. One of his boys in charge of the garage-door-opening ceremony ran over and gave him a hand. Falzarano tried to brush the man off but the man held true to his convictions and got his boss out and on his way.

I watched them disappear through a door that by all accounts led into the connecting passage that led into the main house. While I watched them I reached for the handle of my own door only to find it wasn't where I expected it to be. I turned my head and saw two of the riflemen standing by my open door and the barrel of one of the guns about six inches from my face.

The man behind the rifle smiled and pulled the bolt of the gun with a *clack-clack* and then his finger tightened visibly around the trigger.

13

They took me up an awful lot of stairs. I walked in front and the two riflemen walked behind. I was at the end of their guns, which meant they were quite a long way behind. That suited me. It must have suited them too. I didn't think they liked me and I guessed they wanted me as far away from them as possible. When I'd gotten out of the car I'd made a production out of brushing my tattered suit down, just to give them some idea of how much damage their rifles would do against me.

But they seemed to like being in charge and I wasn't going to spoil their evening any more than it was currently being spoiled by an attempt on their boss's life.

We went up the stairs and eventually the passage opened up into the house proper. I stepped across the threshold and sank to the top of my shoes in a carpet that was the same color as the wine at the Bacchanalian. The house was warm. The walls were a mix of dark wood paneling and finely brushed granite. There were pictures everywhere but of what I couldn't rightly say, just shapes and colors and not much more than that. The light fittings were big and gold and looked more suited to a cobblestoned street being stalked by Jack the Ripper if it weren't for the fact that the glass in them was a peculiar reddish purple color. Call it magenta. The whole place smelled of juniper berries, which wasn't unpleasant.

We walked on.

The place was very quiet. We had the carpet to thank for that. I could almost hear the beating hearts of the two men behind me.

We turned into what must have been the castle's main entrance hall given the huge set of double doors laid with stained glass on our left. The floor here was a black-and-white checkerboard. We crossed it and went through some more doors and back into another carpeted hallway.

After trekking for a while I was about to suggest we make camp and wait until it was light when we arrived at our destination. Ahead were two big double doors in dark wood. One was closed and the other was open and I could see a big room beyond with a low ceiling. The carpet switched from red to green at the threshold but it looked just as thick in the other room. I could see part of a desk the size of a table tennis table and part of Zeus Falzarano as he stood beside it.

I walked through the door. It was a study, or a library, or both. In the corner to my left as I came in was a concert grand piano. Behind it, and all around, the walls were lined with books. There was a scattering of couches in red leather that were studded with buttons in all the right places. There were no windows. The desk was about four-fifths the way across the green carpet and it was as impressive as the folding drinks cabinet that stood beside it. The cabinet was open, the two halves of the top split like an egg and folded down on a hinged mechanism that lifted an array of bottles up for careful selection.

Beside the drinks cabinet stood Zeus Falzarano. He had a drink in one hand and a cigar in the other. The bloodstained napkin was on the corner of the big desk and the gash on his forehead looked pretty angry but at least it wasn't leaking anymore.

Falzarano was talking to two more of his men. Like all the others, they were poured into tight suits and wore equally tight black fedoras indoors. One of the pair had sunglasses on while the other had his pair in his hand. He was flicking one arm open and closed with some level of irritation.

I stopped at a polite distance. Falzarano stopped talking and he took a swig of his liquor as he looked me over. The two men with him looked at me and the guy holding the glasses stopped fiddling with them. His eyes went from me to his boss and back again a few times. Nobody moved. They were well-trained poodles, the lot. Nobody could even breathe without their boss giving the order.

Then Falzarano came up for air and he waved his brandy balloon around.

"Get the hell out of here!" he yelled at the walls. I took it it wasn't an instruction for me because the two men by the drinks cabinet nearly leapt up to the ceiling before rushing out as fast as their tight pants would let them. I heard a variety of metallic clicks and slides and *clacks* from behind me and I turned around to find the two riflemen running out of the room as well. They left the doors of the study open.

I turned back around. Zeus Falzarano was still at the drinks cabinet, making an adjustment to the level in his glass. When he was done he reached down and pulled an empty glass out of the cupboard in the base of the cabinet and he held it out toward me without looking.

"What'll it be?"

Falzarano looked at me and he bobbed the glass in the air. I held a hand up.

"No, that's fine, I—"

"I have a good scotch here."

"I'm sure, but—"

"Of course they say it is brandy, brandy, is what you need for your nerves."

I lowered the hand. Falzarano was bent over the bottles with his back to me.

"I have heard that, sir, but—"

"Now what the hell is this?"

Falzarano shoved his cigar in his face and he extracted a bottle from the stand. The glass was mottled and the liquid inside was bright green.

"Crème de menthe? Who the hell drinks crème de menthe?"

"Well, I—"

Falzarano turned to face me but then I realized he was facing the door behind me.

"Carmina!" he yelled, throwing his head back and his stomach out. He bent back far enough I thought he was going in for a handstand on the desk. "Carmina! Bambina, you been messing around in my study again? Come on, own up!"

There was no reply from Carmina or anyone else. I shifted on my feet and listened to the swish of the thick green carpet. It sounded like waves cresting on a shallow beach.

"So you want a brandy?"

Falzarano's attention was back at the cabinet. I opened my mouth to speak—that is, I opened the little slot that sat behind the grill on the front of my face and my voice synthesizer powered up—but then thought again as Falzarano swung back around to me.

"You don't want a crème de menthe do you?" he asked with a puzzled expression, like I was the one who had put the bottle there and not the lovely Carmina.

"I'm fine, Mr. Falzarano, really." I held my hand up again. This time he seemed to notice. A smile split across his face and he showed me a lot of small white teeth. Then he winked and put the green bottle back and he took the brandy out again. He gave himself another top-up even though his balloon was very much at high tide already.

"Listen, you saved my life back there," he said, all his attention on tipping the bottle by the neck. He sucked his cigar and bluish smoke curled out and clouded his face. "You saved my life and I don't even know what to call you."

"Electromatic," I said. "Raymond Electromatic. But Ray will do, Mr. Falzarano."

Falzarano unleashed a laugh in a single syllable. He put the brandy down. "Ray, Ray, Ray, Ray. Pleased to meet you, Ray. You saved my life back there, Ray, you really did."

"All in a day's work, sir," I said.

Falzarano nodded intently, like he knew exactly what I was talking about.

"Listen, Ray. Me, I don't get to thank people very much.

My line of work, see, I don't have to." He pulled the cigar from his mouth and used it to point at himself. "My line of work, people thank *me*. But you, Ray, no. You deserve it, Ray. You saved my life tonight."

He took a step closer. I was at least eighteen inches taller than he was. Maybe more. He looked up at me and he used his cigar hand to pat my chest. "You, Ray, you get my thanks. You saved my life." He returned the cigar to his mouth. "And, Ray, you gave me an idea. An idea, Ray, an idea!"

I nodded. "Don't mention it, Mr. Falzarano—"

"Zeus, darling!"

The exclamation came from behind me. Falzarano's face froze, and then he sidestepped me and held his arms out.

"Carmina, Carmina, come to your Papa, my bambina!"

The woman at the doorway was young enough to be Falzarano's daughter, but the way she fell into his arms and the way he rested his head against her chest I decided that she was anything but. She had long dark hair that fell to her waist and had honey-colored streaks in it. Her skin was almost as bronzed as my own and I knew that because she was wearing silk nightwear that was split from ankle to hip down one side and from navel to neck up the middle. She muttered to her Papa and stroked his head while he blew cigar smoke across her bosom. She had a deep voice and she muttered in a language in a rich accent that suggested an origin somewhere far south of the United States.

I let the two lovebirds get on with their reunion. I wanted to head back to the office to report to Ada, but I needed to make sure Mr. Falzarano had fallen for the bait first.

I cleared my throat, or pretended to. It sounded like someone grinding the gears in that green Jaguar down in the garage as they tried to back it out.

The green Jaguar.

There was something about that car that rang a bell, but the more I thought about it the more that notion floated away along with a fresh cloud of blue cigar smoke.

"Ah, Carmina, Carmina, Carmina!" said Falzarano as he extracted himself from his lover's embrace. He kept his arms wide apart and he rotated his body a few degrees until it looked like he was going to give me a hug too. "This is the man who saved your Papa's life, Carmina! His name is Ray. Say hello, Carmina!"

Carmina jerked away from her beau and grabbed at the front of her nightie as she turned toward me, acting like she hadn't seen a lumbering robot standing right there in the middle of the room. She scowled and her knuckles bleached as she clutched at the insubstantial fabric, and then she looked me up and down and her attitude changed at once, the fear and surprise I knew to be fake melting away along with her modesty. She let go of the top part of her nightie and it fell open just enough, and then she twisted one leg and her knee found the split and poked out, bringing with it a good acreage of naked skin.

She stood in this pose like she was waiting for me to take a picture for a magazine. Then she swanned over to me across the carpet and I swear she was purring when she got within touching distance.

Either Falzarano didn't notice what Carmina was doing or he did and he liked it, because he chuckled into his brandy and then he pulled on his cigar while his girlfriend twisted in front of me.

"Thank you for saving Old Man Zee," said Carmina. Her

eyes ran me over a few more times. "Tell me, how can I ever repay you?"

I pursed my lips like I'd been practicing and I tried to come up with an answer but then Carmina got very close indeed and she ran the back of one finger along the side of my cheek. As she did so her lips parted and I could see the tip of her tongue. I imagined my skin was cold to the touch but Carmina sure seemed to like it.

"I think, Carmina, we will be seeing a lot more of our new friend Ray from now on, ah, ah, ah?"

Carmina nodded. "I think I would like that, Zeus," she said. "I think I would like that a great deal." Somehow she managed to pull her body away from mine, although her eyes seemed more reluctant to leave. Then she moved back to the old man and draped herself over him again. Zeus wrapped one arm around her waist and then he gave me a little nod.

"Come by at ten, Ray," said Falzarano. "Ten o'clock. We'll talk, Ray, we'll talk about this wonderful new idea!"

I paused. I did some long arithmetic to pass the time. Just for effect. The silence in the room only lasted two seconds but in that time Falzarano and Carmina didn't take their eyes off of me.

"Talk?" I asked.

Falzarano nodded. "Talk, as they say in this country, *turkey*."

Then he drained his brandy and then buried his face in Carmina's neck and he started whispering something that made her giggle. Over his bowed head she kept her eyes on my optics the whole time. Then Falzarano came up for air. "Ten o'clock, Ray, ten o'clock!"

He went back in for a second helping.

I nodded and I turned around and I walked out through the doors. Somewhere behind me Carmina giggled again. I closed the doors and left them to it.

Ten o'clock.

Bingo.

14

I left Falzarano's castle and I drove back to the office. When I got to the hallway outside the office I thought I could smell coffee and before I opened the door I thought I could see someone through the bubbled glass moving around behind my big desk. A woman with big hair smoking a cigarette as she stood looking out the window.

When I opened the door there was nobody there and I knew there never had been.

Then I went through that office and into the computer room. Ada's lights flashed and tapes spun. I took off my trench coat and Ada gave a whistle. I paused, half out of my coat, and then I realized what she was whistling about. I finished taking off the coat and I hung it on the back of the door and I shucked off the tattered remains of my suit jacket and shirt. They dropped to the floor without any fanfare in particular. I stood and looked at them and then I took off my hat and tossed it onto the table.

"So," I said, "how much of this wonderful plan did they actually tell you? I was expecting an attempt on Falzarano's life. I didn't expect the whole restaurant to get blown up."

I had the strangest feeling Ada shrugged. "Well, chief," she said, "whatever happened, happened, and it seems to have done the trick. Zeus Falzarano got scared and Raymond Electromatic got himself a new job. Looks like everything's coming up roses."

I made a humming sound that was similar to a broken air conditioner and I went over to the window. The street outside was lit plenty and despite the hour there was a good amount of road traffic. Life in Hollywood went on despite the loss of its most expensive and most exclusive eating spot.

"I expect it'll make all the papers tomorrow," I said, still looking out the window.

"Oh, I'm sure it will."

"With no mention of Zeus Falzarano."

"Well," said Ada, "why would there be? Nobody had heard of him except the cops and the robbers and neither of them need to read the newspaper to find out what happened."

I made that humming sound again. I liked it. I thought it might annoy Ada so I made it some more. I was trying to tell her I wasn't happy without actually saying it. But I figured she knew what I felt. We were the same computer, in many ways. She was the brains and I was the brawn. Same program. Just different ways of running it.

I went to the closet and opened it. I looked over the shirts and jackets and other things. The shirts were all cream and the jackets were all brown with a yellow pinstripe.

"So Falzarano says he has a big idea he wants to talk to

me about tomorrow," I said, not turning around, not doing anything except looking at all the clothes. "I guess his big idea is me working for him, which is what was supposed to happen. Which means I get inside his house and I get a chance to find out what he's hiding before the client sends his carrier pigeon and I finish off the real job I'm being paid to do."

Ada laughed and sucked on a cigarette that was nothing but an electric dream of mine. "Got it in one, chief."

I frowned on the inside. I picked a shirt at random and got to work.

"Remind me what, exactly, I'm looking for?"

"Well, Ray, come on," said Ada. "How do I know what you're looking for until you find it?"

I'd finished with the shirt. I looked up into the corner of the room. "Why did I know you were going to say that?"

"Because you know me like no other, Raymondo."

I hummed. Ada blew smoke. This time I was the one who did the shrugging. "Okay," I said, and I turned back to the closet. I had five jackets to choose from and they were all the same but I still took my sweet time picking.

Ada chuckled quietly. Maybe she was reading my thoughts. Chances were she just knew me very well and knew the kind of moods I got into.

And chances were that Professor Thornton got into moods just like these ones too and he'd handed them down to me along with every other aspect of his personality.

"So what's the game?" I asked. "What, I just walk in and do what Falzarano tells me?"

"That's about the size of it," said Ada. "You do what he tells you and you keep doing it until we get the word. In the meantime you poke around his house, see what skeletons he keeps in those closets of his."

I nodded. "Any idea how long this is going to go on for, exactly?"

"Nope. Until you find what it is you find. Don't worry about it. For now, you're employed by Zeus Falzarano and you'll like it."

"Okay," I said. I looked over at the alcove where I plugged in each night. I thought about the tapes spinning in my chest and I thought about the shiny new cover over them. I wanted to ask Ada about that, but there was something else pressing on my electric mind. Something was worrying me and now I had a finger on it.

"Falzarano has a big house," I said.

"The lifestyles of the rich and criminal," said Ada.

I looked up into the corner. "Big enough for all his boys to live in—maybe not all the time, but certainly when they're jumpy. Falzarano needs lots of fingers on lots of triggers, and he needs them close by."

"That makes sense."

"So chances are that from tomorrow morning his entourage is going to be plus one mid-sized robot."

"Fingers-crossed, chief."

"One mid-sized robot," I said, "who will turn into a pumpkin if he doesn't come home in time."

A reel on one of the mainframes slowed and I watched as the tape spooled out into a big loop that nearly touched the floor. Then the reel sped up again and the tape snapped back into place.

"These are the facts as we know them, chief," said Ada.

I paused. I made the humming sound again. I waited for

Ada to say something but I had a feeling she was blowing smoke out the window.

"So what happens?" I asked.

Now Ada paused. Perhaps to finish that cigarette. Perhaps to turn from the window and fold her arms.

"That's a deep question, Ray," said Ada. "A little late to be getting philosophical, isn't it?"

I watched the tapes spin and the lights flash. I hummed again. Ada just laughed. "You'll sneak," she said.

"I'll sneak?"

"You'll sneak. There and back. Shouldn't be more than an hour's round-trip. Bad guys are always sneaking around. Nobody will bat an eyelid."

"Or," I said, "their eyelids will be fluttering all the way back to the office. I'm not sure I like the sound of that."

Now it was Ada's turn to hum. "Okay, no problem," she said. "You know how to lose a tail. So lose them. Add another hour's travel. No problem."

I didn't say a word for thirty-seven seconds. I watched the clock above the door. I calculated pi to five thousand decimal places but it didn't do much to cool my circuits. When I opened my mouth grill again I made the humming sound, only this time just a little bit louder.

Ada laughed. I knew she would.

I sighed. It was pretty much the same sound as the humming. "You sure about this?"

"It'll work."

"Are you sure it will work?"

"What, don't you trust me, Ray?"

The first answer to that question that came to mind was yes. But then I thought about my repaired chest unit and I wasn't so sure anymore, so I didn't answer right away. When I did the answer was still yes.

"Time for an early night, chief," said Ada. "You've got a big day tomorrow."

I hummed. "A job interview."

Ada laughed.

And then I stepped into my alcove and plugged myself in and I turned myself off.

15

It was coming up to a quarter of ten in the morning when I cruised between Falzarano's stone lions and past his real life dogs with the real life handlers and cruised the half-mile down to the castle, the sound of Ada's laugh still echoing around my compression wafers after this morning's pickup. When we were done I expressed a few concerns. No doubt I had expressed the very same last night as well, only I didn't remember it.

I didn't need to remember it. I wouldn't have liked the plan last night and I sure as hell didn't like it this morning. The plan made the transistors fizz somewhere around where Professor Thornton's stomach would have been. After the pickup and my complaints, I'd read more of a paperback book that was sitting on the table in the office to try to cool my circuits. Several pages had bent corners. But I started from the start and within a few chapters I felt a little better. If I had a soul I would have said that reading was good for it.

Now as I headed down the driveway to Falzarano's castle I thought more about the plan. The driveway was long and I had plenty of time to do my thinking but I slowed the Buick to a crawl to buy a few extra minutes and I watched the men with the dogs and rifles shrink in my rear view and I thought some more. Then the driveway came to an end: standing in the gravel oval in front of the big fancy fountain were three more men with rifles. Their eyes were hidden behind wraparound sunglasses that were completely opaque, but I knew just what they were looking at.

Me.

And more to the point, those shaded eyes would be looking at me all the time. I was the new boy. I was also different from them. I wasn't expecting my welcome to be warm but I didn't blame them in the slightest. Falzarano's boys were on alert and now their boss's apparent savior was walking among them by personal invitation.

Situation like that, I'd be watching pretty closely too, if only I could find a pair of designer sunglasses big enough to fit around my face.

There were three men in the driveway but there were ten times that number between the house and gate up at the road, and the house in front of me looked big enough to house hundreds.

Which made the idea of sneaking back to the office in the small hours something of a worry. The more I told myself to cross that bridge when I came to it, the more I found myself plotting an escape route.

I killed the car and realized there was another one not

far behind me. A moment later the three pairs of sunglasses hiding three pairs of eyes were pointed away from me and back up the drive.

The other vehicle was small and blue, a two-seater, open-topped. It looked nice and fast but a little small for my taste. The driver had blond hair with a wave and was wearing glasses like the others, but his suit was lighter, almost the same blue as his car.

While I sat in my big Buick the driver of the little car pushed its nose against the shrubbery by the garage just next to me. Then he got out, said something cheerful to the others with a wave that was positively jaunty, and then skipped up the steps and into the house. He hadn't spared me a glance.

I got out of my car more slowly and I said less and I counted the stairs as I took them inside. There were more stone lions at the top by the door, guarding the approaches. They looked annoyed, their muzzles open and frozen in place, eyes narrow.

I knew how they felt.

I stood around inside the entrance hall of the house and looked over the dark wooden paneling that stretched from the checkerboard tiles on the floor, went up the walls and the sweeping stairs that rose on each side and then past the big railed landing that wrapped around the upper part of the hall and kept on going across the ceiling high above, as though the carpenter had got lost in his work and forgotten to stop for lunch. There was a grandfather clock with a pretty painted dial showing yokels shoveling hay into a wagon. What they planned on doing next, I couldn't guess, as there was no horse attached to the wagon. Bit of an oversight.

Of the driver of the other car, there was no sign. Up on the landing at the top of the stairs were more men with guns and sunglasses. They might even have been looking at me. It was hard to tell, but my feelings on the matter were no different now that I was on the inside of the house from what they had been when I had been on the outside.

The grandfather clock's hands moved until they showed nine fifty-nine and then part of the wood-paneled wall in front of me opened and out stepped a woman who Ada had reminded me was called Carmina. Ada had also reminded me to watch her closely, so I started right now. She was wearing a green dress that was cut too high at the side and too low down the front. Her hair was black and long and piled as high as the haystack on the clock face. She had gold bangles on her arms and when she raised her arms to the ceiling they came clattering to a halt at her elbows.

"Ray!" she said with a grin as wide as her cleavage and with an accent as heavy as the gold on her arms. "It is so good to see you! I hope you are well! Please, come with me! Papa is waiting for you!" It was quite a performance, each phrase was a shout, like she wanted everyone inside the house and out of it to know how pleased she was to see me. I glanced up at the landing but the guards hadn't moved any. The front door behind me was still open and I could hear the others walking around on the gravel of the driveway.

I was about to take my hat off when Carmina slid

forward across the tiles and pressed the length of her body against my side. The big slit in the side of her dress had opened up and I could feel the heat of her flesh against my leg. She got herself cozy and got one bare arm up the middle of my back and with a gentle push she shepherded me toward the doors she'd come through and the magical wonderland that lay beyond. As we walked Carmina leaned her head against my arm and she seemed to be softly singing something.

I kept myself to myself. I figured she was Falzarano's lady but inside his empire she could do just what she liked with who she liked and maybe he liked her doing it. I wasn't here to judge. I was here for a job interview.

Through the doors was a corridor lined with more wood paneling and a fine gray granite and laid in a red carpet with a pile so deep it felt like I was walking through sand.

The passage ended in a set of double doors. Our approach had been muffled by the flooring and as we got closer I could hear people talking in the closed room ahead of us.

Then the pressure on my back ceased as Carmina uncurled herself from me and went up to the doors. She stretched out the same arm that had guided me and she knocked twice high on the doors and then without waiting pushed at the middle of them with both hands. Then she pivoted on the toe of a shoe that had a very high heel and made a sweeping motion with her arm that I took to be an invitation. As I passed her in the doorway I braced myself for more canoodling, but she left me alone.

Falzarano's study was how it had been in Ada's pickup— very big, very wide, full of books and big leather chairs and air that was warm and close.

Then the doors clicked shut behind me and I looked at the men in the room and they looked back at me.

Falzarano was there. He was slouched behind his desk like only an old man can slouch. He had both hands locked onto the arms of his chair. On the desk in front of him was an ashtray with a cigar quietly burning on the edge. As I got close I saw that the books on the shelf immediately behind him were different from all the others in the room but were all the same as each other. There must have been a hundred copies of the same book with white spine and red letters.

I Didn't Have Chip Rockwell Killed But If I Did Here's How I Would Have Done It. Zeus Falzarano's magnum opus.

In front of the desk were two men. The one on my left was tall and slim and he had black hair that was swept back from the forehead and shone darkly in the light of the study like fresh tarmac. The light itself wasn't that bright but apparently enough for the man to be wearing sunglasses, which matched the shades of all the other guards I had seen. He was clean-shaven and wore a nice aftershave along with a suit that was tight and narrow in all the right places.

The man standing next to him was the driver of the blue number in the driveway and he would have been the belle of this particular ball had his friend with the sensitive eyes not been showing him up. This close I could see he was tall like his pal but built of more solid stock, with a thick neck sprouting from a shirt that was lime green. It took me a moment to realize he was wearing a tie as well; it was just that it was the exact same color as the shirt. His powder-blue suit was looser and looked more comfortable. This man was blond and his features were rounded but mostly hidden behind a pair of glasses that were a little more practical indoors than those of his friend. They were almost but not quite square and had thick black frames and thick lenses that enlarged his eyes just enough that you were impressed. His hair was pushed to one side to form a series of crisp curling waves that would have made the best patisserie chef in Paris weep into his mistress's bosom. His sideburns were longer than what was fashionable and they had a vague suggestion of orange in them.

Falzarano picked the cigar up and planted it between his front teeth and he slapped the wood of his desk with both hands.

"Ray, my friend, my friend, my friend," he said around his cigar, and then he glanced down at the gold clock that was sitting over in another county on the edge of his desk. "Punctual, punctual, punctual," said Falzarano. "Very punctual. As I expect you to be, my friend. Of course, of course."

I took the opportunity to doff my hat. The man in the sunglasses did nothing except squeeze the wrist he held in front of his belt buckle a little harder. Blondie pursed his lips and I saw his eyes move up and down me behind his glasses. You couldn't miss it. It was like watching television.

Falzarano pulled the cigar out and used it as a baton, pointing out the highlights of the room with the hot end.

"Ray, Ray, I would like you to meet some friends of mine. Gentlemen!"

I looked at the guy with the sunglasses. His lips were pressed tightly together. I couldn't decide whether he was annoyed or whether it was just his general demeanor.

Blondie jerked into life and gave a good-natured chuckle.

"Hello, Charlie! The name's Alfie. Alfie Micklewhite.

But you can call me Alfie. It's Alfie to me mates and we're all mates here, eh? Alfie? All right. All right. How do you do, eh?"

His hand shot out. I took it. His grip was firm and I let my forearm be jogged a few times. With our hands still clasped the man leaned in and spoke out of the corner of his mouth, one hand cupped around his lips as though to keep his conversation private.

"Except maybe Michelangelo here, eh?" said Alfie in a voice that was somehow louder than when he had introduced himself. "He doesn't seem to make friends easily."

Falzarano laughed somewhere behind his desk. Michelangelo—if that was his name—pressed his lips together until they were white.

Alfie clicked his tongue and then he stood back where he had been before. He grinned and looked out at me from behind his lenses.

"Ray," I said. "It's just Ray."

Alfie clicked his tongue again and glanced at Michelangelo. "Oi, cheer up son, might never happen, eh?"

"You're English?" I asked Alfie. This made Michelangelo hiss between his teeth. I glanced at him and saw he was scowling.

"Oh, yeah, yeah," said Alfie. "You know what they say, eh?" He laughed like that explained everything. "Born and bred within the sound of the old Bow Bells." He laughed again then sighed and cocked his head like he was remembering a happy childhood somewhere in what I knew was the East End of London. I had that much on my permanent store, anyway. "Anyway," he said, "a lad has to broaden his horizons, right? Right. City of Angels, the

American West, right? Not to mention the Hollywood dollies. Oh, birds like you wouldn't believe, eh?" He laughed and then the laugh died and he sighed wistfully again and he said "Eh?" again. It sounded like a question but I had no idea what he was talking about. I just smiled on the inside and hoped he could see it.

Maybe he did, because he turned back around to Falzarano's desk. Michelangelo's lips managed to untwist themselves and he turned around too without a word.

I slotted into the middle between them. Falzarano looked up at us and blew blue smoke at the ceiling. He looked pretty happy with himself.

"My friends, my friends," he said. "I'm so pleased you are all here. Alfie, Stefano—Ray is here to join our little family, no? Yes, yes, yes." He gave a little nod at me with eyes half-closed. "We are all a family here, Ray. I think you will be very happy here."

I bowed a little and lifted my hat again. Falzarano's eyes went all the way down to closed. I put my hat back on and wondered if the old man had fallen asleep.

Michelangelo—*Stefano*—shifted on his feet next to me and hissed again like a man disappointed with his race-horse. On my other side, Alfie leaned forward around me.

"Oi, Romeo, what's your game, eh?"

I didn't know what that meant and if Stefano did he didn't respond. Instead he uncurled one hand and waved it at the boss behind the desk and he spoke low and fast in a language I think was Italian. Falzarano hadn't opened his eyes but he was nodding and then he replied to his boy in the same language. So he was awake in there.

I made a note to ask Ada if I could get some foreign

dictionaries plugged into my permanent store, Italian at the top of the list. Seemed like it could be useful for the job.

Then Stefano's head turned and glared at me as best he could with hidden eyes and an expression that was as fixed as my own.

I looked at the boss. "Is there a problem here, Mr. Falzarano?"

Falzarano laughed and he only opened his eyes when he was done. He pointed at Stefano with his cigar.

"Stefano only wishes to point out that he was here first, and that he doesn't need any help from anyone, and especially not from a man of steel."

Man of steel. I liked that. I made a note to tell Ada about it.

Then Stefano spoke again. He spoke for a long time. Falzarano listened and on my other side Alfie seemed to be studying the grain on the boss's desk.

When Stefano was finished, Falzarano shrugged with one shoulder and then the next. He repeated this a few times, like he was weighing up a couple of different options.

"Well, yes, yes, yes, there is a point there, yes, I suppose, yes." He leaned back in his chair. His face lit up and he slapped his desk again. "I tell you what, my sons. You are my family. Yes? You are my boys." He pulled the cigar out of his mouth and made a figure-eight in the air with it. "But we cannot have any feuds in the family. Such things as this are not good for anybody. Okay? I leave it to you to work out, okay?"

Stefano seemed about ready to exhale his own blue smoke. While he vibrated next to me, Alfie nodded at Falzarano, said "righto, guvnor," then unbuttoned his jacket and reached inside.

He pulled out a gun. He held it by the grip and his finger was inside the trigger guard, but he didn't point it at anyone. Instead he showed it to Falzarano.

"Sir, Mr. Falzarano, may I introduce you to Barbara."

Stefano hissed. "Barbara?" he said.

"Oh, so you do speaka-da-English, eh?" said Alfie. He looked back at Falzarano. "Now, sir, Mr. Falzarano. Barbara and me, we've been through a lot together, right? The works. I met her in the war, behind the lines, right, and I have to ask you, sir, Mr. Falzarano, if you believe in love at first sight. Because that's what it was. Right? Love at first sight. The moment I laid eyes on her."

He spoke quietly and slowly with a reverence that was genuine and would even have been moving if it wasn't for the fact that he was talking about an old firearm.

Alfie lifted the gun up and fiddled with it.

"Mauser *Schnellfeuer*," he said in perfect German, "probably 1938, maybe later. Preferred weapon of the Waffen SS. Fully automatic or single shot, you take your pick."

He ejected the magazine, showed it to Falzarano, who seemed only mildly interested, then replaced it and did something else which I suppose made the gun ready to fire. The Mauser looked fairly serious and a little too complicated for such a small weapon. I knew enough about guns but I preferred to not use them, as guns left all kinds of signs they'd been used, the least of which was the hole left in the body.

"Now, Babs here has never let me down," said Alfie, grinning inanely at Falzarano. "Not the once, not ever. She's a little beauty, is Barbara. I'd trust my life with her, I would. Never leaves my side." He laughed. "Sir, I tell you, I even sleep with her under me pillow!"

He looked at the gun. For a moment I thought he was going to kiss it.

Then he pointed it at my chest, and he pulled the trigger.

Falzarano's study was well insulated with all the thick carpet and low ceiling and lots of books and soft furnishings to absorb the sounds of gunfire, but standing next to that little hand cannon it was still damn loud. Louder, given that when the bullets came into intimate contact with my chassis they were bent out of shape and sent ricocheting around the room. Out of the corner of my optic I saw a sliver of bright wood peel off the corner of Falzarano's desk and a couple of books over on the far wall jerked on the shelf.

Alfie fired five shots, each the same absurd volume, each fired at me at point blank range.

Then the gun went *click-click-click* in his hand.

"Oh, bollocks," said Alfie. He lifted the gun, checked the magazine, and pulled something back. Then he pointed it again.

Only this time it wasn't at me. It was at Stefano. The gangster had managed to crack a smirk which now disappeared along with his last breath as he groaned and crumpled to the floor, his tight suit and shirt perforated and both quickly staining with bright red after Alfie sent another five shots into his center mass. Stefano's sunglasses never moved from his face.

I looked at Alfie. He gave a little nod which I thought was more to himself than me.

I looked at Falzarano. He was still sitting in the chair and he seemed pretty comfortable. The cigar was between his teeth and he was grinning around it like a carved wooden carnival head. He nodded slowly and then he brought his big fat hands together and clapped.

"Bravo, my son, *bravo.*" Then he pulled the cigar from his mouth and gesticulated at me. "See, in this family, we fix problems simply, you understand? Now we have the right number of men." He replaced the cigar and chuckled.

I glanced down at my side. My trench coat and suit jacket and shirt were torn and smoking. You could see my bronzed bodywork through the rents in the fabric.

I looked at Alfie. He gave me a smile and laid a hand on my shoulder.

"Oh, well, no hard feelings, eh, Charlie boy?"

I didn't know what to say so I said nothing. I'd been shot at twice in two days and if I could have remembered the first time I would have said it was becoming a drag. That was two suits I'd lost and now I needed a new coat as well. Ada was going to have to break out the petty cash and she wouldn't like that one bit.

Alfie held his malfunctioning Mauser in one hand as he walked around me and knelt down next to Stefano's cooling corpse. Then he unbuttoned the dead man's jacket and reached inside. Stefano had been wearing a shoulder holster, a thing of tooled brown leather that looked as expensive as the rest of his outfit.

Alfie unclipped the business part of the holster and pulled out a gun. It was new and modern, an automatic pistol a good size larger than his precious Babs and far more elegant. It looked well oiled. Stefano had treated the weapon well, only he hadn't felt the need to write it lovesick poems.

Alfie stood up, a gun in each hand. He hefted them both, like he was weighing them up.

Then he tossed the Mauser onto Stefano's body.

"Bloody useless thing," he said. He looked at his boss and lifted Stefano's gun. "I think I'll keep this, if that's okay, Mr. Falzarano, sir. Old Michelangelo won't be needing it no more, eh?" Alfie looked at me from behind his double glazing and he laughed like a drain and when he was done he looked back at his new gun. "I think I'll call her Susan."

He grinned at me. I didn't grin back. I just shook my head a little bit and wondered what kind of psychopath Alfie Micklewhite of East London really was.

Then he snapped his head around and looked at me with his amplified vision. "Here, what's your story, anyway?" he asked. He nodded sideways at the boss without taking his eyes off my optics. "What brings you into Mr. Falzarano's sphere?"

"Ray saved my life!"

I turned to Falzarano and gave a slight bow. Alfie gave a low whistle.

"Stone me," he said. "Saved the guv'nor's life, eh? That little business last night, eh? Stone me."

I opened my mouth grill to speak and then shut it just as fast when Alfie said what he said next, which was, "Thing is, I thought you were a private investigator, like."

I did a few calculations. Then my logic gates flipped and I realized that Alfie Micklewhite was not saying anything that wasn't public record. I was the only robot in town. Of course people knew me. Some people, anyway.

I glanced at Falzarano. His eyes were narrower than they had been before. He looked like he was holding his breath. Weighing the possibility in his mind that he'd made a rather fundamental mistake bringing me here.

Time to play it cool.

"He's right," I said. "I am a private investigator. Licensed and bonded. You can look me up."

Alfie folded his arms. Falzarano returned the cigar to his mouth.

"But last night was lady luck, nothing more. The PI business isn't good for someone like me. Nobody wants a robot but a robot still has bills to pay. So let's just say I'm looking for . . . alternative options."

"Which include working for the other side of the law?" asked Alfie.

I recalled a line I'd read just this morning from the paperback book.

"Let the affairs of humankind lie where they fall," I said. It was a direct quote from the Computer King of Tau Retore, the bit on page nineteen where he gives a big speech to the plucky astronaut hero and his alien girlfriend before leaving them at the mercy of the Beasts of Vega. And while the author wasn't going to be in the running for the Nobel Prize in Literature anytime soon, I was hoping he would at least get me out of a bind.

Alfie smirked and nodded. He looked impressed enough. Then Falzarano clapped his hands again.

"Bravo, my sons, *bravissimo!*" He heaved himself out of his chair and took the long way around the desk before slotting himself between me and Alfie. He looped his arms through our own and turned us around and walked us to the door of the study.

"I love you like you are my sons, yes, my sons," he said. Alfie seemed to like this and muttered something about Falzarano being very kind. I kept my voice synthesizer off.

We made it to the door.

"Listen, I will have a job for you soon, a little errand I will need you to run," said the boss. "But in the meantime, Alfie will show you around. Alfie, find Carmina, she will have a room ready for Ray here. Now, go, and I'll see you later, yes? Yes."

Falzarano sent us on our way with a wave and then he closed the doors.

Alfie and I stood in the corridor. Alfie was still holding his new gun. He looked at it like he didn't know what it was, and then he clicked his tongue.

"Oh, bollocks, I forgot to get Romeo's fancy holster. Ah well." He stuffed the gun into the back of his pants. Then he tapped me on the chest with the back of his hand.

"Now, let's get you settled. You bring any bags?"

"Ah . . . no, as a matter of fact I did not."

"No worries, mate," said Alfie. "We'll find you a room and then we'll see about getting you a new whistle."

He led the way across the sea of carpet. I had no idea what he was talking about but I followed him all the same.

16

The rest of the day at Falzarano's castle passed without incident, or, in fact, anything much happening at all.

Alfie found Carmina. She seemed overjoyed to see him like she had seemed overjoyed to see me earlier and now she couldn't decide who she was in love with more as she led us up the stairs that swept up from the entrance hall and then turned into the big wide landing on the second floor. The landing was almost another room just by itself and was stuffed with furniture and hung with more of the abstract paintings that Falzarano found the need to spend his ill-gotten gains on. There were a lot of doors up here and more passages leading farther off into the house. Four guards with guns and glasses and unpleasant expressions watched us from a distance.

Carmina went up to one of the doors and threw it open with a flourish you might call dramatic. This led to a bedroom that was small and functional in the same way that the Ritz-Beverly Hotel was a roadside flophouse. The carpet here was as thick as it was in the rest of the house except here it was pink. There was a bed that looked a good deal bigger than a king and a wardrobe and some curtains that were pink like the carpet.

I figured Falzarano let his lady friend handle the interior decor.

Alfie stayed in the doorway as Carmina showed me the room. I told her it looked nice. She made a big deal of the bed, going so far as to lie down on it and pull her legs up so the split in her dress fell open and her legs were naked to almost the waist.

I said the room would be fine. She writhed on the bed a little, like a cat stretching out for a nap, and then she said she would leave me to it and she headed out, looping an arm through Alfie's as she went.

Alfie gave me a wink over his shoulder and then closed the door behind him and then I was alone in a room all of my own.

I looked around again. It was bigger than my alcove but all it did was give me the urge to head back to the office. Then I thought the idea of a robot being homesick was a little ridiculous so I reset a few internal switches and walked over to the big window to take a look outside.

The pink curtains were held back by pink ropes hooked onto golden hooks but there were also blinds on the window. I twisted the rod and was presented with a view of a big flat lawn you could have played field hockey on and beyond the lawn were shrubs with waxy dark green leaves and purple flowers that bordered a low wall made out of pale stone and beyond the low wall were tall pine trees made short by the way the property sloped steeply away into the valley. The house sure was well buried in the rugged landscape that loomed over Hollywood. I checked my internal compass and aligned myself at the window and pretended I could see the Hollywood Bowl on the other side of the hill in front of me.

This side of the house was apparently to the west of the entrance and my room looked to be the last of a row. I leaned out a little and looked to my left and saw four more windows like mine. Below each was a wooden trellis painted a dark green and each trellis was wound with the tendrils of a plant that were thick and wet looking.

There were people on the lawn, more of the guards with their guns. Then I saw a hat appear from behind a shrub and float along the top of the low wall before turning around and making the return journey. There must have been a path on the other side, lower than the main gardens, higher than the stand of pine trees. I had a feeling the guy wearing the hat was also carrying a rifle. From somewhere else I could hear a dog barking and a car on gravel. Then the sound was gone and there was nothing but the whisper of the wind in the pines and the buzz of insects in the foliage below my window.

I stood there and drank the view for quite a while. Over the pine trees I could see more Hollywood hills. I could see the appeal. Perhaps Falzarano's pile was too big and filled with too many people carrying guns, but it was the location that struck me. A house in the valley. That was nice. Hollywood was a short drive away but hidden here in the hills it felt like you were on another planet.

Maybe Falzarano did too.

I stood and did nothing. I wanted to call Ada but there was no telephone in my room and I didn't feel like going out to find one with the men outside my door watching me. I figured I'd give them a little time to get used to me before I snooped any. I knew I was a novelty but maybe that novelty would wear off in time.

At three in the afternoon Alfie came back. He was smoking a cigarette and wearing a black trench coat that was short and had a wide belt that was cinched tight and a big collar that was turned up. He said nothing but he jerked his head and then walked out again.

I followed him. We went down the stairs and across the checkerboard tiles and then outside. We got into his car. It was on the small side for me, even with the lid down. But I got in all the same and Alfie made a big show of sliding out of the driveway and spitting gravel all the way. Then we hit the main road and drove out through the hills and down into Hollywood. Alfie kept his cigarette lit despite the wind in his face. He was having a whale of a time too, the way he was grinning and the way he kept pressing his foot steadily harder on the accelerator.

"You like driving, then?" I asked.

Alfie nodded. "Nothing beats it, Charlie. They don't have roads like this back home. They've all run out. No cars like this one either."

"It's a little faster than my Buick," I said.

Alfie laughed. "I'll bet." He patted the wheel. "Shelby Cobra, '65. Bought it secondhand from a little dolly bird, the name of West. Hey, she was a private eye like you! But she was moving to New York. Perhaps she'd had enough of all this sunshine. Or maybe she was looking for *alternative options* like you, eh?"

I frowned on the inside. "I'm sure," I said.

We kept driving and Alfie didn't speak again until we pulled up at an angle outside a store called Jerome's. He didn't actually speak then either, he just got out of the car and I followed and then when he held the door of the store for me he said "Hop along, Charlie, hop along," before throwing his cigarette onto the sidewalk.

An hour later we were heading back to Falzarano's and I was wrapped in a new suit that was a dark blue. Underneath the suit I had a shirt that was purple and came with a tie that was made of the same fabric dyed the same color. On top of the suit I had a short black trench coat that was the same as Alfie's, just a few sizes larger. My brown fedora had been replaced by a number that was identical except it was made of dark-green rabbit felt.

I was starting to like Alfie a little more, even though I noticed he didn't wear a hat. He'd spent a lot of time looking at them in Jerome's with a store attendant at his elbow and I could see on his face there was a genuine curiosity there, but then I could also see that he didn't want to do anything to disturb his hairdo.

I didn't have that problem.

Alfie paid for everything with fresh bills that came off a tight roll of cash and when we pulled back around the fountain outside Falzarano's castle there was a man wearing sunglasses and carrying a rifle waiting for us. He nodded at Alfie and did his very best to ignore me completely. He jerked his thumb over his shoulder.

"Boss is looking for you," he said.

"Ta, mate," said Alfie. He got out of the car and skipped up the steps into the house. I followed a good deal slower and when I passed the man with the rifle he looked anywhere that wasn't in my direction.

That was more like it. I was in a new suit and coat and I had a new hat and I was feeling better about the job already.

17

Falzarano was sitting behind the desk in his study. He wasn't alone. The two seats in front of him were occupied by two men. They sat with their legs crossed in a mirror image of each other. One man had his hands steepled in front of him, his elbows balanced on the arms of the chair, while the other was doing a fine imitation of the boss by gripping the arms like the easy chair was about to be launched like a roller coaster.

The man with the steepled hands glanced over his shoulder at me and Alfie as we walked in and then he snapped his head back around in Falzarano's direction almost as quick. The other man didn't do anything in particular.

I didn't know who either of them was, but the house was full of a lot of people I didn't know. In fact, I had only been introduced to the boss and his lady and Alfie so far and the only other name I knew was Stefano and I knew I wouldn't be seeing him again anytime soon.

I glanced at the carpet by the desk. It was clean but there was a damp patch. Someone had scrubbed up the mess Alfie had left.

"Ray, Ray, Alfie, Alfie, so glad to see my boys again," said Falzarano. We stopped in between the two chairs and I got a good look at the two men sitting down. The one with steepled fingers had a faint tang of alcohol floating around him. He was balding and he had a line of close-cropped brown hair that did one half orbit around the sides of his skull and in the front he had soft, round features and nothing in particular to distinguish himself.

That didn't stop my circuits buzzing as I looked at him.

And then that feeling was gone.

The other guy had short brown hair brushed forward neatly, the furrows left by his comb as deep as a ploughed field. He had a moustache that was trimmed to geometric perfection and he wore glasses with tortoiseshell frames that were a good deal lighter in weight than the apparatus on Alfie's face. He was a pipe smoker and he held a pipe that was short and straight in the corner of his mouth. It looked like it hadn't been lit in a while.

Falzarano nodded at the two men then gestured with both arms stretched across his desk. "Gentlemen, gentlemen, thank you, we will resume our conference later," he said, and then he turned his attention to the cigar box on the desk.

The two men nodded then stood. The man with the round face slipped around his chair and headed out of the office with his head ducked down and his tie loose around his neck. The other guy stood there a moment, the bowl of his pipe cupped in one hand like he wasn't sure his teeth could hold onto it properly. He looked at me, didn't say a word, then left. I watched him go and I watched him close the door behind him.

"Ray, Alfie, please, please," said Falzarano.

Alfie took the invitation and sat down. "Thank you, Mr. Falzarano, sir, thank you."

The leather creaked underneath him. I stood until Falzarano waved again and then I sat in the other chair. The leather creaked underneath me a great deal more.

"I see Alfie has been looking after you, Ray, my son, ah, ah, ah?" Falzarano smiled and clipped the end of his new cigar.

Alfie grinned and pulled his packet of cigarettes out and then pulled a new one out with his teeth.

Nobody offered me anything to smoke. I wondered whether I should short a circuit or two behind my faceplate just for effect.

"Yeah, took him down to old Jerome's," said Alfie. "I'll tell you what, Mr. Falzarano, sir, he got looked after there, I tell you, he got looked after. Lovely chap, that Mr. Humphries. Knows a thing or two, know what I mean, eh?"

Falzarano clapped his hands and laughed. "Excellent, excellent. Now—"

He paused, patting his jacket. He was looking for matches.

I slid to the edge of my seat and I slid a hand forward toward the boss, holding my fingers like I was going to click them. When I was in touching distance of the end of his cigar I upped the voltage and shortened the resistance, the result of which was a blue electric spark that danced on my fingertips. It caught the cigar immediately and

Falzarano sucked hard to get the flame going. Then I sat back and he sat back and he laughed around the cigar while his hooded eyes went as wide as they ever had, which is to say not very.

"Ah, I knew I liked you, I knew I liked you," he said. He pulled the cigar out and looked at the end of it like he'd never seen a cigar lit before.

"Yeah, lovely, wonderful, you're a doll, doll," said Alfie. I turned to look at him and found him lighting his own cigarette with a silver lighter and frowning at the same time. Somebody didn't like the attention being off him.

I sat back in my chair. Alfie pocketed the lighter. Then he reached over to my seat and slapped me on the chest with the back of his hand. He seemed to like doing that. His frown went and was replaced by a laugh which I wasn't sure was genuine. Then he sat back again.

I looked at the boss and got down to business. "You wanted to see us, Mr. Falzarano."

The boss nodded and pulled himself a little straighter in his chair. "I did, Ray. Now, listen, the pair of you. I have a job for you. Something easy, just to get you involved in the business, right, right?"

I nodded. "Sounds fine. I'm sure Alfie can show me the ropes."

Alfie nodded and smoked and lounged in his chair like he was relaxing at his favorite gentlemen's club. He made his favorite clicking noise with his tongue again, like he was trying to talk to a horse.

"Good, good," said Falzarano. "Now, the job, it's easy. I want you to go visit someone."

Alfie blew smoke towards the low ceiling. "That we can

do, sir. Who are we going around to see then?"

Falzarano leaned over the desk, pulling a small notepad toward him with his left hand while extracting a gold pen from his inside pocket with the right. He scribbled on the paper, tore the sheet off, then returned the pad and the pen to where they had been before folding the note in half and handing it across to Alfie.

"Coke Patterson," he said. "An old friend."

Alfie pocketed the note. "Righto, guvnor. You want him, you know . . . ?" Then he made a squelching sound with his tongue against the inside of his cheek and this was accompanied by a stabbing motion, in and out, with his free hand.

Falzarano shook his head. "No, you don't need to go that far, Alfie. All I want you to do is deliver a message. One that he won't forget anytime soon, if you know what I mean." He slumped back in his chair again and shrugged. "Whether he can walk or sign his own name after you leave, that's up to you. Use your initiative, okay, right? But he needs to get the message. Okay? Okay?"

Alfie nodded. I glanced at him and then at the boss. I said, "okay," and Falzarano nodded at me and then he nodded at his cigar, like it was part of the family too.

Alfie came to the end of his smoke and he sat there rotating the last remnants of the thing for fifteen and a half seconds before holding up the spent end. Falzarano grunted and slid a crystal ashtray along the top of his desk like he was serving a drink in the Old West.

"When's kickoff, then?" Alfie asked.

"That I leave to you," said Falzarano, "but I want him to remember your visit, and remember it well, so perhaps very late or very early. Sometime before the dawn, maybe. Use your initiative, okay? Initiative. I need the members of my family to be able to do the tasks asked of them on their own, with only a guiding hand here or there, okay? Okay?"

Falzarano demonstrated this by holding his palms in close parallel over the desk and angling them this way and that like he was shepherding carp in a pond. While he did this I realized he was looking at me.

I was the new boy, after all. I nodded.

Falzarano slumped back in his chair. "Good, excellent, excellent," he said and he slapped the desk with his fat hands again. "I know this job is in good hands. You just come back and you tell Papa how it went, okay? Okay."

Then he returned his cigar to his jaw and he grinned around the smoke.

Alfie stood first, said, "Thank you, Mr. Falzarano, sir, we won't let you down, now, sir." He almost bowed as he spoke and then he gave me a nod and curled around his seat.

I lifted myself out, knocked the edge of my new hat with a metal knuckle, and followed Alfie out. Once the doors were closed and we were alone in the corridor we stood together for a while, Alfie watching the empty passageway with a frown while he patted the front of his jacket with increasing urgency.

"Something wrong?"

"Eh?" Alfie jerked his head like he didn't know I was standing right next to him. "Oh, no, no," he said. "No, the job's a good one. Easy money, as they say. No, we're good, we're good. Peachy in fact. Ah!"

His hand dived behind his lapel and returned to view clutching a packet of cigarettes. Alfie selected one of the smokes and placed the filter between his lips, gazing down the corridor as he did so with narrow eyes shining behind his thick glasses.

I glanced down the hall to see what was so concerning, but there was nothing for Alfie to be looking at in particular, unless he'd taken a dislike to Carmina's taste in decor. A carpet like the one we were slowly sinking into, I couldn't blame him.

"Okay," I said. I checked my clock. It was heading toward six. We didn't have anything to do until dawn, which meant I had time to have a look around the house and then get back to the office and make my report to Ada before coming back to meet Alfie for the job. The timing couldn't have been better.

But Alfie still hadn't moved. I looked at the cigarette in his mouth. Alfie was frowning so hard I thought he was trying to light the thing through sheer force of will.

"So everything's 'peachy,'" I said.

"Yep, Charlie, just peachy," said Alfie. He took the cigarette out of his mouth and then put it back in one smooth motion. "Except I was just wondering, that's all."

"Wondering about what?"

"The job."

"I thought the job was peachy?"

"It is, but them two blokes what the boss was talking to just now, when we came in." Alfie turned back to the doors and pointed at them to make sure I knew which room we had just been in.

I paused. I brought images of the pair back in front of my optics. I looked the man with the soft features over and then I looked at the man with the pipe. "What about them?" I asked.

"Well . . . nah, it's just Mr. Falzarano, right? You know what they say."

"I'm afraid you're going to have to tell me."

"Keep your mates close, but keep your villains closer." Alfie laughed and then the laugh died in his throat and he went back to staring down the passageway.

"You know them?" I asked. I studied the images inside my head. Balding man, soft face, nervous. The pipe smoker, moustache and hair that took some work. I picked the balding man to start. I wasn't sure why I fixed on him first but it was something to do with the way my circuits buzzed again when I looked at his picture, like part of me was trying to get the other part of me to remember something important, something that I had known once but didn't know anymore.

"The bald guy," I asked, "you know him?"

"Eh? Oh." Alfie shrugged. "No," he said. "But I know what car he drives."

I shrugged. "Okay."

"Yeah, a lovely number. Reminds me of home."

"Do tell."

Alfie moved his hands in the air like he was sculpting a woman out of clay. "Ooh, lovely number. Jaguar E-type, British racing green. Import from the old country, right-hand drive. Lovely thing. Lovely."

Something about a green Jaguar E-type made those circuits buzz a great deal more. I had a feeling the bald man with the green car was going to feature front and center in my report to Ada.

"And he worries you?" I asked.

"Oh no, no," said Alfie. "No, not him. The other fella. The one with the pipe."

Pipe. Hair. Moustache. A mean look, but that might have been my imagination running away with me.

"Okay, so you know who *he* is?"

Alfie patted his pockets again, then stopped and turned toward me, angling his neck out like he was looking for a kiss. "Here, be a doll, doll."

I frowned on the inside and lifted my fingers to the end of his cigarette. One blue spark later and Alfie was inhaling smoke so hard his cheeks collapsed right into his face. Then he blew smoke at the ceiling and pointed to the doors of Falzarano's office with his cigarette.

"That bloke with the pipe," said Alfie, "Pretty sure his name is Coke Patterson."

"*That* was Coke Patterson?"

Alfie shrugged. "Think so. Guess we'll find out later, eh?" Then he laughed and slapped my chest again. "Anyway, see ya later, skipper. I'm going to see if I can find meself a bloody cup of tea in this shop." He glanced at his watch. "Meet you in the main hall at, ooh—"

"Four a.m.?"

Alfie grinned. "I like it. Initiative, eh? Initiative. I tell ya, the boss is going to like you. I've got a feeling about it."

Then he set sail across the ocean of carpet and I waited for him to pass out of sight before I headed up to my room, all the while thinking of Jaguars in British racing green and small men with round features that were anything but memorable and what Coke Patterson might have done to incur the displeasure of Zeus Falzarano.

18

If the house was quiet during the day, the thick walls and thick carpet and nothing inside but the slow tick of clocks and the slow footsteps of guards patrolling the carpet and nothing outside drifting in except the faint bark of guard dogs, then at night the house was positively silent.

I spent the early part of the evening looking out of the window of my room, but not at the view, although I might have taken a glance or two in the direction of the stand of pines and the hills beyond now and again. It was a nice view after all.

I had time to kill and a plan to hatch, and that plan had two simple parts.

Part the first, look around the house for whatever it was that our client was interested in. I had to admit that the nonspecific nature of this search annoyed the hell out of me, but I also knew I had to trust in Professor Thornton and the detective skills he and his team programmed me with. I didn't know what I was looking for, but I just had to hope I'd know what it was when I found it.

Part the second, get back to the office so I could report to Ada and get some shut-eye before heading back to work. This was the hard part, and this is why I spent so long looking out of the window. I didn't exactly need to make my coming and going any kind of secret—I wasn't a prisoner, I was an employee, apparently—but nor did I want to draw too much attention to it. Especially given the hours I intended to operate in.

So I stood by the window and I looked out of it. What I was mainly watching was the guard patrols, because these were the men who would see me come and go. That, I wanted to minimize.

So I watched.

From my vantage point I could see several riflemen walking around on the big lawn and several more were down on the path on the other side of the low wall beyond the shrubbery. I learned to tell those guards apart by their hats. The ones on the lawn seemed friendly with each other. Occasionally they would meet and shoot the breeze, figuratively speaking, taking off their hats and wiping their necks with handkerchiefs and occasionally some of the dog handlers would swing by and they'd all have a big old union meeting in the middle of the lawn.

I felt for the guys pacing the perimeter behind the wall. A very late afternoon tea was going on up on the lawn and they knew nothing about it.

What I learned from my hours of observation was that while the place wasn't technically remote, it was hidden enough in the hills to feel like it was, and that, while the place wasn't bounded by a perimeter fence, it was certainly secure enough. If you weren't part of the gang then you didn't get in without an invite, and those who did make it past the stone lions up at the top of the long drive were eyeballed all the way down to the house, and once inside you were rarely out of the sights of a .22 lever-action rifle. Falzarano's little army was doing a fine job of keeping their boss secure.

So far, so good. I figured I could come and go, because I wasn't like the men with the guns. I was part of Falzarano's other little family, those entrusted with "initiative," those who he sent out on personal errands. Let's call it Falzarano's inner circle. The old man had taken a shine to me and I wasn't sure where he had unearthed Alfie Micklewhite from, but he seemed pretty pleased at the team we made. We were even dressed the same now.

That didn't mean Falzarano wouldn't have his eye on me, of course. For all I knew I really was being watched, maybe by the men with the rifles, maybe by Alfie. So I could come and I could go but there was more than a fair chance my movements beyond the walls of the castle would be watched and reported on.

Which meant I had to be careful. But I knew how to lose a tail. So long as I picked my moment I was fairly sure I could make my way back to the office in West Hollywood without much of a fuss. I considered my period of careful observation at the window of my room to be time well spent. Soon enough the day grew dark and I watched as the lights down by the bottom of the trellis outside my window and the lights buried in the shrubbery by the low wall came on and lit the whole building up like it was the residence of the French ambassador and not that of the most infamous criminal mastermind on the West Coast.

A few moments after the outside lights came on I heard a humming sound and the lights all dimmed, just a little, all at once, before coming back up to full strength. That number of bulbs was bound to be a fair draw on the power. Either the main city supply up here in the hills was running through old thin lines that took a moment to adjust to the increased load, or Falzarano was running a generator that had to do the same.

I waited a little longer, counting the ticks of my internal chronometer to pass the time and the ticks of the old house cooling in the evening air. The lights stayed nice and bright.

Then I got to work.

I pulled the blinds and then I pulled the curtains and in the dark I walked across the room until I got to the bedside table. There was a light on it that was a thing of gold and glass that looked like it belonged in the Louvre. I turned it on. It cast a warm glow. If anyone came by the passage outside my door they'd just figure I was reading my paperback book.

I moved to the door. I listened at it. There was no sound from the other side. I reached for the door handle, and then I heard it, and then I stopped.

It was music. Piano music, faint but with a clarity that didn't come from a record or a radio. I opened the door a crack and the sound of the piano got a crack louder.

Someone tickling the ivories in Falzarano's study. It was a slow and steady tune that was neither happy nor sad nor particularly memorable and whoever was playing was good but not that good. Maybe that was how Falzarano relaxed after a hard day sitting behind his big desk, smoking his cigars and handing out assignments to scare old friends of his to death.

Bully for him.

I headed out in the corridor and closed my door. I turned and checked how much light leaked out from underneath it. It was good enough.

I looked both ways and then I picked a direction and headed toward it.

19

I made a left and then a right and then I walked some more and started hoping for a street sign, because navigating Falzarano's castle was turning out to be a royal pain in the posterior geometric field stabilizer and the decor was rich and stuffy and it all looked the damn same to me. I wished I'd picked up a wool sweater at Jerome's because at least I'd be able to unravel it and leave myself a trail back to my room. But I didn't have a sweater so I had to make do with creating a three-dimensional integrated vector-plot field map as I went instead. That would do just as well as a piece of thread.

The place wasn't empty but that didn't mean I saw anybody. I heard talking and laughter behind closed doors and I saw shadows moving in the light cast from within. There were people in the house but I stayed out of their way. The guards were still creeping the carpet but there seemed fewer of them in the night shift. Even a hood needed his beauty sleep.

Whatever I was looking for, I thought Falzarano's study would be the place to start the search. According to the house plan I was drawing up, the room was a windowless box set more or less at the center of the whole place. Nice and secure. A place to keep secrets.

The problem was that it was not currently unoccupied. Someone was in there playing the piano. Maybe Falzarano himself, although he was an old man and it was late and I had always figured that old men went to bed early.

I walked on and aimed for the music. It had been with me the whole time as I moved around the house and it sounded like it was somehow following me, coming and going like the ebb and flow of a tide, the wood paneling and the thick carpet doing strange things to the acoustics of the place. But with a little concentration and a few adjustments to the vector plots in my head I got a fix and I soon found myself back where I had started on the big landing above the entrance hall. Falzarano's study was down the stairs and through the door and down the long passage.

My return must have coincided with the intersection of several guard patrols, because now the landing was home to five men with rifles. Two had their backs against the balcony railing across from me and were talking in low voices, their faces lit by the red glow of cigarettes as they smoked and chuckled quietly. Their rifles were leaning against the rail next to them.

On the next side another guard had sat himself on a wingback chair big enough for the queen of England to recline in with a little whiskey sour. I watched him get comfortable with his hat pulled down low over his eyes and his rifle laid across his knees. Nobody else seemed to mind but I wasn't sure Falzarano would be pleased to see one of his precious boys asleep on the job.

There were two more men and these ones were doing what they were supposed to be doing, which was patrolling the house. They were on opposite sides of the landing and as they walked they looked down into the entrance hall, their gazes as slow as their strides.

I did as best a job I could of holding my breath and then I walked out into the open and wheeled around toward the stairs. There may have been a quicker way to Falzarano's study from here but I didn't know it.

The reaction of the guards was nothing to write home about. The two men huddled in their cute little chat looked up briefly then returned to the conversation. The patrolling riflemen may have glanced in my direction but I didn't notice. The fifth wheel snored in his chair.

This was good news for me. As I had suspected, any interest in the new boy had evaporated already. So long as I was in the house, anyway. I still thought I'd have some eyes on me once I got *outside*. If I were the boss I'd trust the new boy only so far myself.

I wasn't at the stairs before one of the doors on the balcony swung open, and sharply too, the man on the other side of it hanging onto the doorknob for dear life as his eyes fought for some kind of focus.

The door in question was right by my elbow and the man clutching it jerked back and then his gaze focused somewhere in the air above my head. I stopped and I saw that the guard nearest me had stopped too.

The man used the entire length of his forearm to scratch under his nose and I saw his knees sag as he got a better grip on the doorknob. He was the balding round-faced man, the man from Falzarano's little conference, the one Alfie said drove an E-type Jaguar in British racing green.

The man that made my circuits buzz like a wasp nest that had just been given a good hard poke.

He was still wearing his suit and it looked like he'd been sleeping in it. His tie was still in place but the knot was steadily heading south. His jacket looked stretched out on one side. There were socks on his feet and drink on his breath.

"Hey, you, you!" he said, loudly at first and then his eyes went wide and he looked around and he exhaled, short and shallow. "Come here, come here," he said, in a stage whisper you could have heard down on Sunset Boulevard.

He stayed in the doorway and gestured for me to come closer, each wave of his arm causing his whole body to rock. By this point all the guards who weren't asleep were looking in our direction and the one nearest had stopped just a few feet away. He looked amused.

I moved closer to the man in the doorway but not much. He nodded with some vigor.

"Listen," he said, "can I go now? I mean, really, thanks a whole lot, but I have things to do, you know? Places to go and people to see. I'm a businessman, you know? I have work to do. A lot of work. Mr. Falzarano is going to be real annoyed if this doesn't go through, okay? I mean, really, this place is swell, it is really, but you know."

Then he stood tall and he puffed his chest out. His cheeks were doing a fair amount of puffing as well.

"Look, I'm a busy man, a busy man," he said. "I'm

important. A V-I-P." He patted his chest and grinned and then went back to huffing. "The old man, he knows that, and listen, you can say thanks to him but no thanks from me, okay? Okay. Good. I have work to do. I have to go to work."

Then his gaze shifted and he saw the guard standing not quite beside me. The man's eyes narrowed and his brow furrowed and his voice went up a few decibels.

"Hey! Can I go now? I need to go now. You tell the old man, okay? Okay."

He swayed in the doorway and he looked at the guard and then he looked at me and then he looked at the guard again. He swayed again. He had gotten his drink on and it turned his face into a cartoon of emotions. He scowled at the guard, and then that scowl turned into a leer.

"You think you can keep him safe with that kind of hardware?" he said. "They had *machine guns*, bub. Machine. Guns."

Then he let go of the door knob and he bent his elbows and mimed the restaurant shootout, his lips flapping and a good deal of saliva ricocheting like bullets off the sideboard next to his room.

Then he slumped his shoulders. "Ah, forget about it. You don't understand a word, do you? Stuck in a house full of them, I am. A whole damn house full."

"Keep it quiet, Ellis," said the guard with the rifle in an accent that was pure sun-kissed Californian. "I'd be happy to let you walk out that door, but I don't think the boss would be too happy when we drag your dead body off the road and into his office, now would he?"

Ellis.

My circuits buzzed and I had no idea why but it sounded pretty important.

Ellis mumbled something, and then he sniffed and looked at me like I was the one who had spoken. "Okay, fine, you've made your point. But listen, you just have it all ready to roll, okay? Okay. We can have it all set up, no problem, but the longer I'm here, the longer the old man has to wait. And he don't like waiting, do he?"

He was still looking at me. He looked at my face and his eyes crossed. Whether he even knew I was a robot or not, I couldn't tell.

"Alfie?"

I shook my head. That answered my question.

"Ray," I said.

"Hey, Ray, have a nice day, okay?" said Ellis. He gave the guard a glance.

I knew Ellis was important to me and I wanted to find out why, so I turned around and gave the guard a nod. "I've got it," I said. The guard sniffed and looked at me. Then he turned and walked back to his patrol route, only stopping once to look over his shoulder at us.

I pushed Ellis a bit farther back into his room. He had replaced his grip on the doorknob with a grip on my arm. He leaned in and spoke in the whiskey-soaked stage whisper again.

"I don't like those guys," he said. "I don't like guns. Too many of them around, you know what I mean?"

I watched the guard's back as he moved away from us.

"Yeah," I said. "Actually, I think I do."

"Right. Anyway. I need a drink! Dammit, I need a drink and you need a drink. Do you want a drink? Let's get a drink. Oh."

The piano played on somewhere in the house.

"Oh?" I asked.

"I've run out," said Ellis. "They don't make bottles like they used to, do they?"

"Ah, no."

"Get me a new one." Then Ellis pawed at his mouth with one hand and then he grinned and nodded. "Oh, listen to that, listen."

We listened. I watched Ellis. He closed his eyes and lifted his chin and did something with his fingers.

He was listening to the piano.

"Nice tune," I said.

"Oh, nice *lady*," said Ellis. "Hey! She has the key to the old man's liquor cabinet, Alfie. Say, say, you go down and you send her up here and send her up here with a bottle, okay? Okay. And then we'll have a little drink."

"Yeah, okay, I'll do that," I said, and I began to gently push Ellis back some more. He let me push him and his Oscar-winning leer reappeared. I pushed him inside and toward the messed-up bed and he sat on it still leering and then he fell onto his back with his arms outstretched. He hummed something that was a vague approximation of the piano tune but only just.

I watched him for a whole minute. His eyes were closed and he seemed to have forgotten I was there.

"You're important, Mr. Ellis," I said. "You're important and I don't know why."

He might have heard me, the way he hummed and smiled. But his eyes stayed closed.

"You want to tell me why you're important?"

The humming began to fade and a moment later the snoring began.

"I guess you don't," I said.

As I left the room I closed the door behind me. The guard reappeared at the end of the landing. I knocked a finger against the brim of my hat and the guard did the same and then went back to his patrol.

I turned and headed for the stairs, following the music all the way and thinking that the important Mr. Ellis had just given me an excuse to get myself alone in Falzarano's study.

20

The doors to Falzarano's study were closed. The piano was loud out in the corridor so I knocked with volume on the dark wood. The piano didn't stop but a woman's voice said, "Come in!"

I pushed the doors open and walked in.

"Ray, darling," said Carmina. She was seated at the piano and was playing it while lifting her arms up and waving them around in a way that didn't look very efficient. The music bounced off the books and the couches and the thick carpet in a way that would be pleasing in a concert hall but in the low-ceiling room was too loud. You wouldn't be able to work in here with all of that going on. Maybe that was why Carmina waited until Falzarano was in bed before she came in here and practiced.

I eyed the desk. It was big and it had lots of drawers that looked good enough to hide lots of secrets in.

Then I eyed the drinks cabinet next to the desk. It was a big wooden thing on a big wooden pedestal and locked with a big brass lock. If I could get Carmina out of the room I could have a good sniff around while Falzarano was counting sheep.

I made it halfway to the desk when Carmina stopped playing. There was a clunk. I turned around and found her now draped against the study doors, which she had apparently closed with the length of her body. She was wearing a silky dress in a burnt orange that did wonders for the tone of her skin, which I could see an awful lot of thanks to the split down the side and the split down the middle.

"Better not disturb the others, Ray," she said, and she said it over her shoulder and from underneath a long strand of hair and when she pushed herself off the doors and sailed toward me the hair stayed just where it was. She had the tools and she knew how to use them. I could see that, even though I was a robot who had no firm opinion one way or the other on the allure of beautiful women.

But that allure was a tool. Like the dress. Like the hair. You didn't move around in the world she did without knowing what you were doing and with whom you were doing it.

"I'm sorry to disturb you, Miss—"

"Carmina, please. All my boys call me Carmina."

Of course they did.

"I just came down to get Mr. Ellis something to drink."

Carmina was within touching distance and touch she did. The fingers of her hand played up and down my left arm.

"Emerson Ellis is a pig," she said quietly. "The sooner he is out of here, the better." Her fingers trailed off my arm and across my chest as she walked over to the drinks cabinet.

"Why is he here, then? He doesn't seem like he wants to be part of Falzarano's little family."

Carmina looked over her shoulder at me. "Oh? What's he been saying?"

The question and the move that went with it were both designed to be innocent, a passing interest, nothing more. But I'd been a private detective once and I was programmed to recognize that kind of body language when I saw it. She only wanted me to *think* she wasn't particularly interested.

I had no real idea of who Carmina was, but she interested me. She was more than just Falzarano's companion. Maybe she kept some of those secrets that I was supposed to find out about.

"Nothing much," I said, "only that he's fed up of being in this house and he wants to go home. He claims to be a very important person." I ended with a shrug.

Carmina pursed her lips. "Maybe he is, maybe he isn't. I don't know. That's Papa's business. All I know is that Ellis is doing work for him. He was here often."

Now it was my turn to do some of that playacting. "That so?" I asked in a way that suggested I was more interested in the contents of the drinks cabinet Carmina was resting one hand on.

"Then one night he came in, and he hasn't left yet."

I *hrmmed*. "He must like the way you mix a cocktail."

A smile appeared somewhere near Carmina's mouth. "He was drunk when he arrived."

"He's doing his best to keep up appearances right now."

Carmina laughed. "I told you, Emerson Ellis is a pig."

That didn't stop her from working on the drinks cabinet.

Finally it opened and she looked down at the contents.

"This business he's doing," I said, "for Mr. Falzarano. Any idea what it is?"

"No," said Carmina. She was still looking down at the bottles and she really did sound like she couldn't have cared less. That may have been true, but I had a feeling that her answer just now had been anything but.

"Must be important," I said. "I mean, important enough that Mr. Falzarano doesn't want Ellis out of range. Maybe he's in danger and Falzarano is keeping him safe. Until the job is done, I mean."

Carmina extracted a bottle from the cabinet and turned back around. She caressed the bottle and she seemed extremely interested in the label on the outside of it.

"I was told you were a private investigator," Carmina said to the bottle.

I shrugged. "Once upon a time."

Carmina dragged her eyes up to my optics. The smile was still there somewhere but it was getting harder to spot. "Seems strange, Papa hiring you to protect him."

I shrugged again. "Maybe," I said. "Or maybe he sees my worth."

The smile reappeared over the horizon like a rising sun. Carmina moved closer to me and as she did she moved her shoulders in a way that made the front of her dress spread itself open just that little bit more. She took a finger and planted it on my chest.

"Oh yes, he sees your worth," she said. "We all do."

I glanced down at the bottle of whatever it was, now sandwiched between my chassis and her bosom.

"The pig wants another drink, and if he's so important to

Mr. Falzarano then maybe we should humor him."

Carmina looked up at me. Her hair fell back in front of one side of her face, right over her left eye. "You sure you don't want to join us?"

I held up a hand. "Thanks for the offer. Maybe next time."

Carmina sighed, the expression dramatic, the act back in force.

Then she swooshed across the carpet, bottle swinging, and left the study, and when she turned around to close the double doors behind her there was a sparkle in her eye and in the instant before she was gone I could have sworn those eyes moved up and down.

Finally I was alone. I went to the desk and started looking.

21

Somewhere I heard the clink of a spoon against a ceramic mug, but when I looked up from the table all I could see were Ada's computer banks, a thousand lights flashing in arcane sequence, a thousand miles of tape racing from one reel to the next. Above the door that led out to the main office, the clock's smooth second hand cruised ever onward. In one minute it would be midnight.

Four hours until I was due to meet Alfie. Four hours until we were due to put the frighteners on Coke Patterson.

I'd struck lucky in Falzarano's office. Once Carmina was out of the way I'd waited a few minutes. I killed time by reading the titles off the spines of all the books that lined the walls of the room. There were eight hundred and thirty books on display and a quarter of them were duplicate copies of Falzarano's own blockbuster.

His hulk of a desk had nothing on the top of it but a blotter and the crystal ashtray and the telephone and the small pad Falzarano had used earlier. I'd checked the pad but it was clean, not even an impression left on the top sheet.

The underneath of the desk had been more interesting. The thing was fitted with more pullout storage space than the average family home. There was one big long drawer that ran just about the full width of the desk. It had a big lock with a tarnished brass escutcheon that wouldn't have looked out of place pinned to the chest of a war hero.

I'd stopped and listened a moment but heard nothing from beyond the doors. Carmina was in another part of the house so I'd gone for broke and pulled on the big long drawer. It had slid open without a sound.

What I had found in that drawer I'd laid out on the desk and taken pictures of with the twin cameras behind my optics and now those pictures had been printed at the office and were laid out across the table.

I looked up into the corner of the room the way I always did when I wanted to make sure Ada was watching.

"Interesting," I said.

Ada laughed. "So cool and modest too. I knew I liked you, Raymondo."

I looked back down at the pictures. "I'm guessing this is what we were after?"

"I'm guessing you're right, chief."

The photographs were black and white, but the original papers had been blue. They were big, rectangular papers, covered in fine white lines and tiny white text that popped against the deep dark background. The papers had been so big I'd had to stand tiptoe just to get a good shot of them.

They were blueprints. They'd just been sitting in

Falzarano's unlocked top drawer. I pointed this out to Ada and she tsked. "What happened to hiding a safe behind a picture on the wall? Don't the bad guys keep stuff in safes anymore?"

I shrugged. "What does he need with a safe or a locked drawer when the whole house is under armed guard?"

At this Ada laughed. "Little does he know his pet robot snoops for a hobby. He's going to be annoyed with himself when he ends up dead."

I rearranged the photographs on the table and resumed my inspection, tracing the lines on one of the plans with a bronzed steel-titanium finger.

The blueprints included building plans as well. There was a diagram of one big building that was long and boxy. The plans showed the building in various elevations and at varying levels of detail. I pushed that picture away and dragged over another. This showed something else, a smaller building with a neighboring area surrounded by a high fence. The blueprints for this place showed the development with the fence both in situ and removed to show what lay behind it, which was detailed on another sheet. Looking at this one I tried to make sense of a series of big boxy constructions covered in pipes and fins. There were other things too, poles wrapped in coils and tall pylons with cables. The scale on the blueprints told me these things were fairly big, like small buildings in themselves.

"So what is all this?" I asked. "It's big. Not just one building, but a whole lot in a cluster. Looks industrial, maybe a factory or warehouse?"

"Got it in one, Ray."

I tapped the picture of the boxes and coils. "Whatever

he's building looks like it will need a lot of juice," I said. "This could be plans for his own electric power station."

Ada's purr filled the whole room. "As you said, chief, interesting stuff."

"And what else is interesting is this," I said. I pulled one of the pictures off the bottom of the pile and tapped it. It was a close-up of one of the corners of the blueprints, showing a boxed block of white text. The same block was stenciled into the corner of each sheet of the plans.

"Prepared by Emerson Ellis Building and Construction."

"Well, that makes sense," said Ada. "You want to build a factory, you hire the best commercial developer in the city."

"Emerson Ellis," I said. "The same Emerson Ellis Falzarano is hiding inside his house."

If Ada took a sip of coffee I wouldn't have blamed her given the hour. I knew she was a night owl. I also knew she was a computer and she didn't drink coffee and just like that the image and the sound vanished.

"Well, he has a good reason to hide," said Ada, "and that reason is you."

I pursed my lips, or it felt like I did. I'd been doing it a lot lately. It felt good. It helped me think.

Of course I was the reason Emerson Ellis was in hiding. I didn't remember him but some other part of me did and had been trying to tell me all this time.

"The Jaguar," I said.

"Pardon me?"

"He drives a Jaguar. Green thing from England. Very nice. I parked next to it this morning and I thought it rang a bell. And that bell has been ringing ever since."

"Huh," said Ada. "Another memory fragment on your

tape. I'd say your system needed another overhaul, but these little flashes seem to come in handy sometimes."

I was going to ask what she meant about *another* overhaul, but then I knew about how she had reprogrammed me to be a killer and I also knew about the new cover on my chest. I must have put that on myself, under her guidance, after something happened to the old one.

"So Emerson Ellis was another job, then?" I asked. "Except that couldn't have gone too well given that he's still alive and well and has Zeus Falzarano's lady friend plying him with liquor."

"He's our open case," said Ada. "You went looking but he'd gone to ground. But at least we know where that ground is now."

"Okay," I said. "Now we know where Ellis is. You want me to see to that job too while I'm there?"

Ada *hrmmed*. Beside me the tapes on one of the big mainframes spun one way and then another and the lights flashed in sequence. Ada was thinking.

I went back to the pictures. The plans were crawling with text outside of the corner boxes, all of it technical, a lot of it measurements of length, height, angle. Then I noticed another block, one on each of the plans, this time circular instead of square, positioned at the top corner of each sheet, the exact place varying a little. The text was black and a little hard to read against the dark of the blueprint paper but I managed.

"Application approval oh-eight sixty-seven," I read. "Vaughan Delaney, Department of City Planning."

"Now there's a funny surprise," said Ada.

"Don't tell me," I said. "Another name I knew once."

"That's right, chief. Another job. Only unlike Ellis, Vaughan Delaney is dead."

"Glad to hear it."

"Only you didn't kill him."

"Oh." There was no denying I was a little disappointed.

"He did the deed for us."

"*Oh.*"

I looked back at the photographs. I rearranged them again, like it made any difference. "So let me get this straight," I said. "Falzarano wants to build a factory and a power station. He hires Emerson Ellis Building and Construction. The plans are approved by Vaughan Delaney, city planner."

"Except if the one and only Zeus Falzarano is into real estate, you can bet there's something fishy about it," said Ada. "Chances are he doesn't want anyone looking at it too closely, so he greases a few palms to make sure it all goes through without a fuss."

"One such palm belonging to Vaughan Delaney."

"Well, he did have a very nice car."

"Only once the plans were approved," I said, "Vaughan Delaney dies by his own hand?"

"Apparently so."

Something about that didn't feel right. "Except he didn't. He couldn't have."

"I'm listening, chief."

"Vaughan Delaney dies and that spooks Falzarano, so much so he grabs Emerson Ellis and hides him away. The reason Ellis is so upset about it is because he's not at Falzarano's castle voluntarily."

"Oh really? He said that?"

"Ada, the guy would have told his life story to a potted

palm tree if you put a hat on it. He'd just downed a bottle of scotch and was looking for another. All he said was that he was very important and that he was grateful to Falzarano but that he wanted to go, and he wanted to go now, because he had important work to do."

"I get it," said Ada. "Delaney didn't commit suicide. He was killed and it was made to look that way."

"Right. Because with Delaney out of the way, whoever succeeds him will no doubt review his recent permits. Instead of being quietly filed away in a dusty vault somewhere underneath downtown, with the city planner himself on hand to obfuscate proceedings as needed, Falzarano's plans will come out in the open."

"Good word that, Raymondo. 'Obfuscate.' I'm impressed. I must remember to use that in casual conversation."

I frowned on the inside. I think Ada knew I did because she laughed. I glanced down at the plans again.

"So whoever our client is," I said, "they want to stop Falzarano from building his factory. We were hired to take out Delaney, Ellis, and now Falzarano. The client knows the three of them were doing something, something big— big enough to kill each of the players to stop it. But they weren't entirely sure what that something was."

"Hence the arrangement to get into Falzarano's place and find out."

I whistled. I looked out the window. The blind was up and all I could see was myself and the computer room around me reflected in the black glass.

"The client has resources and know-how," I said. "They arranged the restaurant hit. That kind of thing couldn't have been easy."

"They have deep pockets, that's for sure," said Ada. "You were following Vaughan Delaney nearly a month, and let me tell you, your hourly rate has a tendency to make the eyes water."

"That's interesting." I gestured at the photographs on the table. "You think this is all they want?"

"I'll check and let you know. That's good work, Ray."

"Thanks," I said. "Ellis. He's a weak link. If I take it softly I think I can get him to spill a little more on these grand plans."

"Great idea." Ada blew more smoke around my circuits. "Keep him alive for the moment, see what you can shake out. Now, about that other job."

I looked up into the corner of the room. "The other job?"

"The one Falzarano has for you. What was that guy's name again?"

"Coke Patterson," I said. "Seems like he is—or was—a close associate. Alfie says he's been around Falzarano a while. That's all I have. He's done something to annoy the old man but I don't know what."

"Okay," said Ada. "You're heading out at four, right?"

"On the dot. I'll take forty winks and a new tape before I go back."

"Okay, good. Plenty of time. But first things first."

"First things first?"

"Won't take long. When you're done there'll be time to come back and get a new tape, then you can go on your playdate with Alfie."

I stacked the photographs on the table. I squared the edges, squeezed them tight.

"What won't take long?"

Ada took a puff of her imaginary cigarette. "I have a little job for you."

22

I have to say I liked Hollywood at four in the morning. It was quiet. Those who had gone out for a night on the tiles were either already home or were locked in for the long haul. It was still a couple of hours before the working crowd stirred and the nightshift was still beavering away.

Four in the morning was a good time for certain deeds. I liked four in the morning.

I wasn't sure my companion could say the same. The Shelby Cobra had the top up and I sat in the passenger seat while Alfie Micklewhite sat behind the wheel, and between yawns as wide as the Grand Canyon and the continual sweeping of one hand over his hair as he tried to flatten his blond curls into his signature look he managed to keep us more or less on the right part of the road. There was hardly any traffic to bump into nor many parked cars to swipe so we were safe enough and we made good time. The traffic lights were all asleep, their middle orange lights blinking, blinking, blinking, like we were a plane coming in to land and they were guiding us down onto the runway.

"I don't suppose anywhere in this bloody town will do a decent cup of tea at this time of the morning," said Alfie. He yawned again and his eyes remained shut for so long I thought about reaching over and taking the wheel. Then he was back in control and pushing at his hair again. He glanced at me. "You fancy a cuppa, Charlie?"

"No, that's okay," I said. I kept my eyes on the road. "You sure you know where we're going?"

"Of course I bloody do." Another yawn. "The Pacific Breeze apartments. Number 12D. I know where I'm bloody well going. Pacific bloody Breeze. Honestly."

"Sorry for asking," I said.

The Pacific Breeze building was an Art Deco wonderland that consisted of a tall oblong with rounded edges that went straight up to catch the air it was named after. The outside of it was crawling with sunray motifs and arches and other bits and pieces that people in the 1920s seemed to like carving into every available flat surface. The building didn't have much in the way of grounds but what it did have was filled with so many palm trees I wondered if Alfie had remembered to bring the machete and mosquito nets.

We parked out back. There was nobody around and the sun was still a ways from making its appearance. Once we were out of the car Alfie seemed to wake up, his expression set, his whole body somehow tighter, full of a sort of springy energy, the eyes behind his big glasses now the steel gray of the dusty sidewalk.

We went in the back through a loading door Alfie picked

the lock of without much difficulty but with plenty of cursing. Inside the Art Deco theme continued. The corridors were lit with sconces decorated with chrome sunray moldings. The carpet was red and edged with gold and was thin but it muffled our footsteps well enough. We went up via the service elevator because we didn't want to meet any early risers. The service elevator was so ornate I almost wanted to take the risk and have a look at the one designed for the residents.

Apartment 12D was a door identical to all the others in the hallway. White wood with gold trim and gold hardware. Alfie picked the lock of this door with a great deal less swearing while I kept watch. The building was certainly nice and I discovered I liked Art Deco, as faded as that particular glamor was here. The building was fairly narrow on the outside so I figured the apartment beyond the door Alfie was working on was probably equally small and narrow. There were probably a dozen buildings just like this within throwing distance.

Alfie opened the door. I was right. The apartment was nice but small and it was full of stuff that was packed into it in such a way that suggested the place was really not quite big enough but that's just what you put up with if you wanted to live in this part of the city but you didn't have money like Zeus Falzarano had money.

I closed the door behind us and the light from the corridor vanished and we were left in darkness. I turned my optics up but then realized Alfie didn't have the knack for that so I reached for a table lamp and turned it on and then I reached for the frilly silky thing that was on the back of a nearby chair and I threw it over the lampshade. That plunged us into a red-tinted glow that for some reason made me think of a sinking submarine.

Thornton again. I'd never thought about submarines before, let alone ones drifting into the abyss. Maybe he'd been in the navy.

Alfie moved like a cat through the apartment, which is to say he turned and twisted his body around occasional tables and side tables and easy chairs and dining chairs as he navigated his way to the back of the place. The only pieces of him that touched anything were the unmarked soles of his shoes.

I was bigger than he was but I was good at moving around without anyone knowing I'd been there, so I managed well enough. Maybe just a little slower.

There was a hallway at the back of the apartment with doors coming off it. Bathroom. Cupboard. Another cupboard. Then a third. They were probably pretty handy for storing your illicit moonshine back in the days of flappers and Prohibition.

The hallway ended at another door. Alfie was standing next to it when I came up to him. He had his shoulder against the door and his ear too and one gloved hand was ready on the doorknob. My logic gates clicked and told me this was the single bedroom and that behind the door Coke Patterson would be asleep, pleasantly unaware of his nocturnal visitors and the message they brought from mob boss Zeus Falzarano.

Alfie looked at me, gave me a nod, and then opened the door. The room beyond was darker, but I could see a bed and something in it.

Alfie went in. I followed. And then I stopped and

watched because I had a certain feeling about what Alfie was about to find. I didn't know what it was. Just the way my circuits buzzed.

There was just the one body in the bed. The covers were heavy and looked orange although that might have been the weak light coming in from the shaded lamp all the way over in the front room. There was a crocheted throw on top of the blankets and the body underneath it all lay on its back and was covered right up to the neck.

The heavy orange blankets and the crocheted thing were as still as I was. But Alfie didn't seem to notice. He walked up to the head of the bed, leaned over the body of Coke Patterson, and brought his nose right up to the other man's.

"Coke Patterson," said Alfie, his lips pulled back into a rictus grin, his heavy glasses in serious danger of sliding right off of his nose, "you are a bloody dead man. Wake. Up."

He punctuated those two words with a hefty stab at Coke Patterson's chest. The chest that hadn't moved ever since Coke Patterson had stopped breathing who knew how long ago.

"Oi!" said Alfie, as loud as he dared, which was plenty loud enough. "Patterson! Get the hell up. We need to have a little chat."

More stabs of the chest. Then Alfie stood up and looked down the length of Coke Patterson's body. Then he looked at me.

I reached down and grabbed the heavy blankets and pulled the lot off the bed and onto the floor in a single motion.

Coke Patterson lay on the bed in an undershirt and boxer shorts and nothing else. The sheets underneath him were rumpled and were white apart from the patch on the left side that was a much darker color. In the dim bedroom the circle of color looked brown but I knew it was probably a dark red.

Alfie folded his arms then readjusted his glasses then refolded his arms. "What the bloody hell is all this then, eh? Eh?"

I pointed at the bed. It seemed unnecessary but it gave me something to do. "Seems like someone got here before us."

"Well I can bloody well see that, can't I?" said Alfie. He sighed and fiddled with his glasses again.

I looked down at the body. I couldn't tell when the man had died but he looked pretty fresh. I moved around to the other side of the bed and pulled a bit at his stained undershirt. There was a hole in it in the side and underneath that was a slot cut into the man's side in a corresponding position.

"Knife to the kidneys," I said. "Somebody knew what they were doing."

"What, and he just lay there and let them have at it?"

I looked around. There was a nightstand on either side of the bed and on the one nearest me there was a wide shallow glass with a little clear liquid in it. Beside the glass was a pill bottle. I picked that up first and unscrewed it. It was empty. The label on the outside had Coke Patterson's name printed on it along with his address. Alfie was watching me, so I tossed him the pill bottle and then I picked up the glass.

"Sleeping pills," he said.

The liquid in the glass was vodka. I told Alfie. He nodded.

"So our friend Coke had trouble getting his kip, then?"

"Which made it easier for the killer to come in and slice him in the side."

Alfie shook his head and he tossed the empty pill bottle onto the bed. "Well, this is a right bloody to-do, isn't it? Mr. Falzarano's going to be over the moon, isn't he? Dance a bloody jig he will."

I put the glass back down on the nightstand and was glad I couldn't leave fingerprints. "I think we should go," I said. "All we can do is tell Falzarano what we found."

"Yeah, well, right you are, Charlie," said Alfie. I looked at him. He still had his arms tightly folded. He seemed fairly annoyed at the death of Coke Patterson. Alfie had been cheated of his morning fun.

Then Alfie shook his head and he slid out of the apartment and I followed and a few minutes later we were driving into the sunrise of another beautiful day in Hollywood, California.

23

We drove the dawn streets in silence. I was lost in my thoughts and I imagined Alfie Micklewhite was lost in his.

I had no idea who Coke Patterson was or what he had done to Zeus Falzarano to earn an early morning visit from two of his boys, but I imagined Alfie was right, the old man wasn't going to be pleased. Not that it was anything to do with us. All we could do was go back to the big house and tell the boss what we'd found.

The streets were getting busier already and the traffic lights had switched back to their daytime sequence except for the set in front of us, which were as dead as Mr. Patterson back at Pacific Breeze. There was a policeman in the middle of the street wearing a white covering over his hat and big white gloves that came up to his elbows. There was a whistle in his mouth and he was blowing it with some enthusiasm as he directed traffic. It was always a pleasure, seeing someone really enjoying his work.

"Course we never had robots in England," said Alfie. He had one wrist resting on the top of the wheel and the other one was busy managing the cigarette he was smoking. His window was cracked to let the smoke out but all it was doing was letting cold morning air in.

"That so?"

"Yeah, sure," he said. He pointed through the windshield at the policeman. "You fellas used to have them all over the shop, right? That was you directing traffic once upon a time, eh?"

I frowned on the inside.

"And I heard they was all over the place, running trains and busses and the like, delivering the post, collecting the rubbish. Sorry, *garbage*." He turned to me. "Or is it trash? Honestly, the way you bloody well garble the mother tongue, it's hard to keep track." He turned back to the windshield. "Still, must have been a right lark, eh?"

I ran his words through my processor a few times to do a little translation of my own before I felt qualified enough to answer his question correctly.

"Well," I said, "that was a little before my time. But you're right. Once upon a time there were robots. And then there weren't."

Alfie sucked so hard on his cigarette I thought he was going to swallow it. "So how comes you're still here, then, Charlie?"

"I was the last robot out of the factory," I said. "I was supposed to be the first of a new generation, but as soon as I stepped out the door the whole federal robot program was cancelled. They shut down the Department of Robot Labor and that was that."

The policeman pointed a giant white glove in our

direction and waved us on. Alfie stuck the cigarette in his mouth and worked the gears and we lurched onward. Alfie gave the cop a wave as we went past.

"And, what, they just let you hang about the place and become a private detective?"

"They did. Too much money had gone into me and my computer so they let our program continue as a sort of experiment, to see if a robot really could live independently in the real world. Private investigations was what they programmed me for so private investigations it was."

"You learn something, Charlie, you learn something."

I wasn't sure if Alfie was joking or not. He was concentrating more on driving one-handed and smoking his cigarette than listening to me.

Falzarano's place was a little way away yet so I changed the subject.

"What about you? What brought you to the States?"

"Oh, the usual," said Alfie. "I wanted to be an actor."

"You wanted to be an actor?"

"Yes, that's right, Charlie, I wanted to be an actor. Blimey." Alfie glanced at me like I'd just insulted his mother. Then he returned his attention to the road. "I'd been doing odd jobs around the place back home but I got fed up with the weather and decided to move on. And where else do you come for the glitz and the glamour, eh? The City of bleeding Angels is where, my friend. And I tell ya, what a town this is, eh, eh?"

We began to climb the hills and I studied the road ahead.

"So how did an actor become a heavy for a man like Falzarano?"

Alfie grinned. His cigarette somehow stuck to his bottom

lip and flapped around as he spoke. It was quite a trick.

"Oh, well now, you see, turns out acting isn't quite my bag, right? On account of the fact that I'm bleeding diabolical at it. Course I didn't know that at first. Looks easy, right? You just pretend to be someone else. Not very hard. Except it was bloody impossible. Anyway, found myself at something of a loose end, Charlie. A loose end. Also, I didn't say what those odd jobs were back home, now did I, eh?" He shrugged and wrestled with the wheel. "Anyway, Alfie, I thought to meself, Alfie, why don't you do what you're good at, eh, lad? So I asked around and got myself a nice little position with Mr. Falzarano. Know what I mean? How did you put it? Alternative options? Eh? Well, there you go. Found meself an alternative option."

I nodded. I didn't remember saying that but that was just business as usual so I believed him. Alfie looked at me and he laughed, and then the cigarette fell off his lip and onto his lap.

"Oh, bloody Nora!" Alfie scrambled to retrieve his lost smoke. He looked down and he dragged the hand on the wheel with him and we crossed the centerline. The hill road was quiet but another car was coming back down and we were pointing right at it.

I grabbed the wheel and pulled it back toward me. The other driver was quite within his rights to lean on his horn and he did so heavily.

Alfie looked up and he had the cigarette back in his mouth. He said thanks around it, gave me a wink magnified by his glasses, and we continued up the hill.

"No problem," I said, and I held my breath the rest of the way.

24

Falzarano took the news better than I thought he would, which is to say he sat in his chair behind his desk with his eyes closed and first Cuban of the morning filling the air around his head with blue smoke that was so thick I couldn't even see if the old man was breathing or not. So far he'd only uttered a single syllable, and that had been the "well?" that had been spit out as soon as Alfie and I parted the carpet en route to his desk.

On the way in Alfie had told me to do the talking, but standing in front of the desk, all he did was twist his mouth without making any words. The fingers of his right hand flickered in front of his belt, like he was getting cigarette ash off them, while with his left hand he worked on his troublesome coiffure.

I did the talking. Just the facts as I knew them. I tried to keep it simple and I think I succeeded given that I didn't know a heck of a lot to begin with.

When I was done Falzarano didn't speak. He didn't open his eyes and his cigar was literally going up in very expensive smoke.

Alfie sniffed and turned to me and made a shape with his mouth. Then he shrugged.

I thought Alfie made a good point.

And then the doors behind us opened very quietly and were shut with the same volume.

"You've done well, my boys."

I turned and watched Carmina walk toward us and I wondered why she was whispering. A moment later that seemed the lesser of two mysteries when Falzarano jerked into life behind his desk.

"You've done well, my boys," said the old man. He smiled and sucked on his cigar and his eyes glittered behind the smoke. In the meantime, Carmina continued her slow way toward the desk. She took the scenic route, around the piano, her fingers trailing over the ebony surface. Then she hit the bookcase and her fingers were now at head height, conducting a survey of the tomes by touch alone.

"It can't be helped," she whispered.

"It can't be helped," said Falzarano at a rather more elevated volume.

"As far as I am concerned, you did the job that was asked of you," she whispered. Falzarano repeated the phrase.

My attention was torn between the two of them. My face was immobile, given that it was made entirely of metal, but Alfie was doing enough expressions for the pair of us.

"I will call for you when I need you again." Carmina was at the desk now.

Falzarano sat up. He leaned forward and lowered his cigar onto the edge of the crystal ashtray, balancing it just so. "I will call for you when I need you again," he said. He was looking at us as he leaned and he kept on leaning. He was as frozen as I was.

Carmina walked around behind him, and laid her arms across the old man's shoulders. If he knew she was there, he didn't give any indication.

Beside me Alfie rolled his shoulders. Then he stuffed both hands into the pockets of his jacket and he stuck his elbows out and he gave a little bow.

"Right you are," he said. He used one of his protruding limbs to nudge my arm. Then he turned and left.

I looked at Carmina and I looked at Falzarano. The latter didn't move and the former gave me a very small smile but she didn't take her eyes off me.

Out in the corridor I closed the doors behind me. Alfie was absently searching his person for something to smoke but he stopped when he saw me.

"Well then," he said, "that was all right then, eh?"

If I could have raised an eyebrow I would have. "That was all right?"

"Well," said Alfie, "he doesn't seem too worried about Coke Patterson, does he? Seems like someone got in before us, did the job, eh? No problem."

"No problem? If I were the boss I'd think that was very much a problem."

Alfie cleared his throat and resumed his search for tobacco. "Yeah, well, I was just looking on the bright side, eh? He says it's okay, it's okay. Okay?"

"Except he didn't say it. She did."

Alfie froze again, hands in the middle of patting down his own jacket. He glanced at me sideways from behind his plate-glass glasses. "Yeah, I noticed that. Odd, innit?"

"That's one way of describing it."

"Here, it's early, maybe he didn't get his kip, eh? Maybe she was just giving him a few, y'know, prompters. Yeah, that's it. That's it. I told you, he looked a little peaky. Not getting his kip, that's it."

I *hrmmed*. Alfie jerked his head back at the sound.

"As a matter of fact," I said, "you told me no such thing."

"Yeah, well, you know what I mean."

I stood and watched Alfie locate his cigarette and ignite it with his own lighter. While he did this, I heard a humming sound rise and fall from somewhere behind me. The lights in the hallway dimmed a little in perfect synch. A moment later the humming stopped and the lights came back on bright.

I glanced at Alfie, but he didn't seem to have noticed. He was too busy examining the burning end of his cigarette.

"Speaking of kip, I'll see you later," said Alfie, and with that he walked down the hallway and disappeared around the door at the far end.

I waited in the corridor. I looked at the lights in their sconces on the walls. They didn't dim again.

Then I decided to have another little chat with Emerson Ellis.

There was a guard outside Ellis's assigned room. I nodded at him and he nodded at me and then as I raised a metal knuckle to knock on the door the guard just gave me a shrug so I knocked.

"Mr. Ellis?" I asked the wood of the door at very close range.

There was no response. I tried again, the knock and the question both a little louder. Still nothing.

I stepped back and looked at the guard.

"Is Mr. Ellis in there?"

The guard shrugged. "Well I saw him go in, bub," he said. He had a bad attitude that came with wearing sunglasses indoors, and I was pretty sure I was far from being his bub. "And I sure as hell didn't see him come out."

"He have any visitors?" I asked. Carmina would have been a little hard to miss, although now that I thought about it I hadn't seen the guard outside the door the last time I'd come this way.

The guard shrugged. He was getting good at it. He'd clearly had lots of practice. "He's probably passed out," he said. "Damn fool is a drunk, you ask me."

I hadn't but the guard was right. Emerson Ellis had looked a little seedy back in Falzarano's study and he had gotten a lot seedier the last time I saw him. Falzarano might have been covering his accommodation but I wondered if he was going to make Ellis pay for his bar tab.

The guard sighed and didn't quite shove me out of the way, but I could tell he wanted to. Instead he thumped on the door with the bottom of a fist and he yelled down at the doorknob as he did it.

"Hey! Ellis! Wake up, you got a visitor here!"

We both waited. There was no reply. I turned my audio receivers up but I couldn't hear anything over the breathing of the guard at my shoulder and the tick of the watch on his wrist.

The guard looked at me. His lips were a little apart and while I couldn't see his eyes I could see his eyebrows as they peeked out over the top of his narrow black glasses.

I jerked my chin at him. "You're supposed to be looking after Ellis for Mr. Falzarano, right?"

The guard nodded.

"So I suggest you check on him, because the old man isn't going to be too pleased if anything happened to his houseguest right under his nose. Nor will he be happy to hear about how the men he pays to guard his guests disappear off into the night when they should be up here wearing holes in the carpet."

The guard gritted his teeth and he gave me a nod. Then he slid his rifle down to lean against the wall and he fumbled with a set of keys that hung on his belt. Eventually he found the right one and unlocked the door and we went inside.

The room was full of everything it had been last night with the exception of Emerson Ellis. I walked around to the foot of the bed and followed the twisted pile of sheets that spilled out over the bedstead and over toward the big window that looked out over the big lawn by the side of the house.

The sheets didn't quite reach the window but the window was open. The guard had got there ahead of me and he was leaning out.

"God dammit!" he muttered, and then he pulled himself out. "Goddamn idiot went down the trellis," he said as he passed me at speed. "I'll let the others know. We'll have to search the grounds."

He left and I was alone in the room. I went to the window and looked outside.

The guard was right. The trellis below Ellis's window wasn't quite true to the wall. The tendrils of the plant climbing it were bent and broken, and a little farther down two of the wooden struts that made up the crosshatching were broken, the pale yellow wood at the splits showing up against the dark green paint.

Emerson Ellis had said he wanted to go home, and it looked like he'd made his break. I turned back to the room and looked at the bed. He'd tried the old routine of tying sheets together, but had abandoned it once he realized he had a perfect ladder right outside. On the nightstand next to the bed was a half-empty bottle of scotch and there was an empty one down on the floor beside it.

I heard raised voices. I turned back to the window. The big lawn was filling up with guards, the one from outside Ellis's room now coordinating his pals. Soon the guards were pointing this way and that way and they were nodding to each other. A couple of patrols with Dobermans showed up and were sent merrily on their way.

That Ellis had gotten past the guards patrolling outside was interesting. Maybe he'd been watching their movements from his window just like I had. Maybe he hadn't been quite as drunk as he had seemed.

I left Ellis's room and I headed for the stairs. Before I even got close I saw Alfie rattling up them two at a time.

"Here, there's a right flap on, and no mistake!" he said. His eyes were wide behind his glasses and his chest moved up and down from the short burst of unexpected exercise.

I hooked a thumb over my shoulder. "I know. Ellis is out."

Alfie's labored breathing paused for a second and he stood up a bit straighter.

"Eh?"

"Ellis," I said. "He's made a break for it. Climbed out his window."

Alfie grimaced like an eyewitness to a road traffic accident. "Eh? No, mate. It's one of the guards."

"What about him?"

"He's dead, mate."

I felt an amplification coil begin to get a little hot somewhere under my collar.

"What?"

Alfie turned and pointed somewhere in the opposite direction to Ellis's room.

"They've found him out in the bloody bushes is what! Bloody well killed he was."

Alfie turned and raced down the stairs. I followed.

So much for Emerson Ellis sneaking quietly past the guards.

25

"What a to-do," said Alfie, drawing long and slow on his cigarette. "What a bloody to-do."

We stood together on the topmost step of the many that led up to Falzarano's front door, collars up against a breeze that was stiff but by no means cold. It didn't stop Alfie shivering inside his suit. And I didn't blame him. We stood there and watched as men with hats and guns moved around the gravel driveway below us, talking, pointing, a fair amount of nods and even more shakes of the head signifying something, anything, nothing. All this went on while the big fountain carried on its show with the dead guard laid out on the gravel behind it. His gun was beside him. His sunglasses were still in place. His arms had been drawn up so his hands were clasped over his chest like he was on show down at the local morgue.

He was dead. I couldn't see any blood. I wondered how

Ellis had done it. Maybe a rock to the back of the skull. There were plenty of rocks around, in the garden and in the trees and at the edges of the driveway. That's how I would have done it. A rock to the back of the skull in the middle of the night and nobody would know until you were a long, long way away.

Beside me Alfie shivered and smoked and shook his head while he smoked.

"Didn't think he had it in him," he said.

I frowned on the inside and nodded on the outside. Alfie was right. Emerson Ellis was small, soft. The dead guard was a head taller and made of stronger stuff.

Clearly everyone had misjudged the little real estate magnate.

"You say he climbed out the window?"

I nodded again. Alfie held his cigarette out at arm's length and considered it very carefully.

"Bloody cheek," he said. "It was only a bit of protection, wasn't it? Eh? The old man was just keeping his business interests in order, weren't he, eh?"

"I suppose he was," I said. The breeze shifted and Alfie's smoke got in my optics.

"I mean I don't blame him," said Alfie. "Not after the last fella. Now there was a scene, and no mistake."

I raised a metaphorical eyebrow. Out on the driveway the men with guns had thinned a little, looking for clues in the undergrowth no doubt. What they really needed was a private detective. "The last fella?"

Alfie nodded. "Yeah," he said, his eyes scanning the scene before us. "I tell ya."

I said nothing. Alfie smoked.

Then I said, "You tell me what?"

"Oh! Well, now." Alfie leaned in toward me. "I tell ya. There he was, and then there he wasn't, eh?"

Then Alfie did something a little strange, which was to lift his cigarette hand high in the air and stick his thumb out. Then he turned his fist so the thumb was pointing down, and he brought the fist down, all the while making a whistling sound that wasn't a million miles away from the sound you'd expect a bomb to make when it was sent on its merry way to ground zero.

"Bang," said Alfie. "There it was. Jumped out of the bleeding window, he did. Sixth floor, so I heard. Smashed up his motor too. Shame about that."

"Yeah, real shame."

"It was a nice car."

"I can imagine."

Alfie smoked. While he smoked I thought about a few things.

"This guy who took a dive," I said, "his name wasn't Vaughan Delaney, was it?"

"Oh yeah," said Alfie. He sucked the cigarette, seemed satisfied that he had extracted its full worth, then tossed it over the side of the stone steps. Then he extracted a lighter from one pocket of his black trench coat and a packet of cigarettes from another and soon enough he had another one kindled. "Another of the old man's business associates. Worked for the city, I think. Planning department or something. I don't know. Mr. Falzarano had him on the hook for something."

I nodded. Alfie knew something. How much, I had to find out.

"So Falzarano is into real estate now?" I asked.

Alfie shrugged into his collar. "No idea, mate." He paused. "Don't think it was real estate. The old man had a hand in manufacturing, I think. Think he was going to build something. A factory, maybe. I don't know. Nothing to do with me, mate. But whatever it was, someone found out something and old Vaughan Delaney decided to take a shortcut from his office to his car."

Alfie smoked. And then he turned to me. "Here, what's with the questions, eh?"

I looked at Alfie. His big eyes moved over my face from behind the magnifying lenses of his glasses.

I shrugged and I made a point of turning back to watch the men with guns do nothing in particular down in the driveway. "Nothing in particular," I said. "I was just wondering. Ellis is in the construction trade too. No wonder Mr. Falzarano wants to keep a close eye on him, after what happened to Delaney. Keeping a close eye on his business interests, like you said."

"Yeah, well, yeah," said Alfie, and he said it like he absolutely knew that to be the truth.

I thought about Coke Patterson. I had no idea who he was or what his relationship with Zeus Falzarano had been. Falzarano had wanted him frightened, not dead, but dead he was and neither Alfie nor I had laid a finger on him.

And neither, apparently, had we laid a finger on Vaughan Delaney, and Vaughan Delaney was also not frightened but as dead as Coke Patterson. Only Vaughan Delaney had done the job to himself.

Hadn't he?

And now the third party, Emerson Ellis, was gone. I was

amazed enough that he'd made it down the trellis without breaking his leg or even his neck but I was more impressed by the way he'd been able to take out one of Falzarano's handpicked house guards.

I guess that whoever had first said that appearances can be deceiving had been a wise man indeed.

One of the guards down below looked up at us and said something and waved at Alfie. Alfie shivered and looked at me, like I needed to give him permission. But give it I did, with a nod that was returned in kind. Alfie trotted down the stairs toward the others.

My presence was clearly not needed. Which was fine by me, because I wanted to do a little bit of that private detecting I'd used to be so good at. There was one person who didn't fit into the story, and that person was Coke Patterson, and I didn't know if it was important or not but I wanted to find out.

And that was what I was supposed to be doing. I was inside Falzarano's organization in order to find things out.

With Ellis gone and one guard dead, I thought I should do my duty and report to the boss. I only hoped he was a little more awake than last time.

Because while he was my boss, at least for the moment, there were a few questions I wanted him to answer.

26

On my way to Falzarano's study I passed some of his guards. They were all heading outside and they all carried rifles and they all moved quickly, their eyes hidden behind their sunglasses, their lips pressed tight. I didn't need to see their eyes to read their mood. One of their comrades had had his ticket punched and it seemed like Emerson Ellis had been the one to punch it. Now Falzarano's entire organization was moving to find him.

The boss was going to be in a hell of a mood, which was good news for me, because it meant he was distracted, and distracted was good because when you asked people things when they were distracted they tended to say things they normally would want to keep to themselves.

At least that's what my programming told me.

In the hallway to Falzarano's office I was suddenly alone. The doors ahead of me were closed. The silence was deep enough to swim in, and my footsteps on the thick carpet added precisely nothing to it as I moved to the doors and stopped outside them. I listened. I heard nothing. I opened the doors.

Falzarano's office was empty.

I stepped in and I closed the doors and I looked around. Okay, Falzarano wasn't here. He was somewhere else. Supervising. Telling people what to do. Telling people to find Emerson Ellis and to hell with the consequences. Wanted, dead or alive. Although preferably alive because he had a factory to build.

Or perhaps Falzarano had gone back to sleep and it was Carmina giving the orders. That possibility seemed like a fairly distinct one to me. Falzarano was an old man. Carmina, his love, was at least thirty, forty years younger. As far as I could tell, Falzarano's boys paid her as much respect as they paid him, which was to say an awful lot.

So yeah. Carmina knew what she was doing all right.

I looked around. There were a lot of books, and the piano, and the easy chairs and a couple of smaller occasional tables around them, and the rug, and the big desk. I'd already done the desk. There was nothing on the occasional tables and while it was possible there was something hidden underneath the rug I didn't much feel like getting down on my hands and knees to take a look. Not just yet anyway. My attention was on the books and on the shelves that held them. You could hide a lot of things on shelves like that. Hell, you could hide a lot of things in the books themselves. And that wasn't even counting the possibility of secret doors, hidden compartments, books that weren't really books and shelves that weren't really shelves but portals to valuable caches of information, of data.

I frowned. There were a *lot* of books. I lifted my hat from my head then I put it back down again as I calculated how long I wanted to risk turning the office over. It was going to be a big job and with all the fuss over Ellis and the dead guard I figured my time was relatively short. I was alone in the office at the moment but that was a stroke of luck I didn't want to lean too heavily on.

Ahead of me, about one nautical mile away, sat the telephone on the edge of Falzarano's desk. It was the only telephone I'd seen in the house so far. I thought this was a good time to use it.

"Ray, it's been an age!" said Ada inside my head as I listened to the roar of the ocean coming through the earpiece. "You never write, you never call. A gal gets real lonely, Ray."

"It's been all of two hours."

Ada made a sound that suggested she was more interested in stirring her coffee than discussing the finer points of timekeeping. "So what's cooking, chief? You got something for me?"

"Maybe yes," I said, "maybe no." I filled her in on the events of the morning, from Coke Patterson to Emerson Ellis to the demise of the guard. While I spoke Ada hummed like she was taking notes and then when I was done she puffed on something that might have been a cigarette.

"Okay," she said. "Interesting times, Ray, interesting times."

I curled the cable of the telephone around my hand as I looked around the empty office.

"I'm in the old man's office now. I'll see if there is anything else to be found, but I'm starting to think that

Falzarano keeps his secrets locked in his own head. Or maybe Carmina is the one with the secrets." I told her about the little scene with her and the boss, when Alfie and I had reported back after the Coke Patterson job.

Ada made a cooing sound. "Aw, Ray, you're doing well. You're doing really well! Let me do some digging, see what comes up."

"You think Carmina is important?"

"Oh, you'd better believe it, chief, you'd better believe it."

Then the lights in the office dimmed and the room was filled with a low humming. I looked at the ceiling, my audio receptors taking readings. By the time the humming had stopped and the lights had come back on I had frequency, amplitude, a decibel rating. I also had something of a direction.

I turned and looked at the bookcase behind Falzarano's desk, the one filled with nothing but copies of his own book.

"Mission control to Raymond Electromatic, come in, Ray!"

I lifted the mouthpiece back to my mouth. "Sorry. I just found something else to look into."

"Atta boy, chief."

"Gotta go."

I was short of time so I killed the call. As I put the phone down I thought I heard Ada laughing and then I was alone and the office was silent once more.

I walked around the desk. The room was rectangular and the wall behind the desk, like the wall with the main doors opposite, was one of the short ones. The shelves ran all the way across. They went from the floor to the ceiling. They were home to Falzarano's prize collection.

I Didn't Have Chip Rockwell Killed But If I Had Here's How I Would Have Done It.

I looked. I listened. There was no humming. There was no sound at all. The air was still. There was no breeze to suggest a secret passage, unless it was very well sealed, if not hermetically so.

I turned around. The lights were shining bright and steady.

I thought again about the humming. It was a power draw, a strong one, the drag too big, the main fuse board of the big house straining against the load. And it wasn't just an increased load from the lights outside. I couldn't see them from Falzarano's office because Falzarano's office didn't have any windows, but it was daylight outside. Had been for hours.

As I contemplated this fact there was a click from behind me and a whoosh of air and another click. I went to turn around but I heard a woman purr and then I heard something with an infinitely higher pitch and then and then

And then

And then

And then and then and then

And then

And then I woke up and it was another beautiful day in Hollywood, California.

27

I looked around the office. Ada's lights flashed and her tapes spun. Across from my alcove the rise of the morning sun cast long shadows on the brown building opposite ours.

I heard . . .

I heard nothing. I reset my audio receptors. That didn't work. I went to step out of my alcove and then and then and then

!!PROGRAM BREAK!!

And then
And then

!!PROGRAM BREAK!! **** ERROR 66 ****
SYSTEM RESTART IN 5 . . .

And then

4 . . .

* * *

I woke up and it was another beautiful day in Hollywood, California. Just like it always was in this part of the world. Around me Ada's lights flashed and her tapes spun. Across from my alcove the rise of the morning sun . . .

Somebody spoke. It was a woman. For a moment I thought it was Ada but then the voice spoke again and I knew it wasn't her. It was deeper, the accent unusual and thick. The voice was also low, furtive, annoyed. The voice was talking to someone else and they were both somewhere behind and below me, like they were standing behind me, bent over as they examined something on my chassis.

Which was impossible, given the chassis in question was hard up against the back of the alcove.

I went to step out of that alcove and then and then and then

```
!!PROGRAM BREAK!!
```

And then **** ERROR 66 **** and then and then

```
                              **** ERROR 66 ****
                              **** ERROR 66 ****
                              **** ERROR 66 ****
```

And then

```
!!PROGRAM BREAK!! **** ERROR 66 **** SYSTEM
RESTART IN 5 . . .
                    4 . . .
                    3 . . .
```

I woke up and it was another beautiful day in Hollywood, California. Just like it **** SYSTEM RESTART SUCCESSFUL END LOOP END **** always—

"No, no! See? Here and here, okay? Try again."

"If you could get your bleedin' fingers out of the way, maybe we could actually get this thing off! Just let me—"

"No! *Ay! No estar bueno!*"

"Oi! Language, please! Any luck?"

"It's sealed. I don't have the right tool . . . I just need to . . ."

"*Ouch!* Gordon Bennett!"

"Careful, you idiot!"

"All right, all *right!* I know what I'm bleedin' well doing!"

Then a scrape. Metal on metal. Fingers on blackboard.

Then more talk, low and fast and hurried and nervous and annoyed. The woman muttered in a language I didn't understand but which I thought was Spanish or maybe Portuguese. The other voice was male and all it did now was huff and whistle and hiss.

And then a new sensation. A soft pawing, gentle strokes, then something sharp skittering across my chassis. Then I felt a numbness that was hard to describe considering I was made of metal and metal didn't feel anything, not really. What I had were sensors for air pressure and temperature and all that jazz and they were telling me something only I wasn't awake enough to listen.

Wasn't awake enough.

I opened my optics. I looked around. I saw the office. I saw Ada's lights flash and the tapes spin and then they weren't lights or tapes but they were books. Lots of books, on lots of shelves. There was a grand piano in the corner. A big set of double doors in dark wood.

I knew where I was. I had a feeling. Only I—

I didn't remember.

There was a click, then a crack.

"Well, that's bloody well gone and done it, hasn't it?"

The woman swore and I'd had enough.

I went to step out of my alcove that I knew I wasn't standing in and then and then and then

And then

   And then

      And then and then and then

**** ERROR 66 ****

          **** ERROR 66 ****

                    **** ERROR 66 ****

The room wasn't dark. The light on the nightstand was on. I watched the light for a while. I don't know why.

I was standing in my room, the one Falzarano had allocated to me. The bed was made. My short black trench coat—Alfie's pick—was lying on it. The room was quiet. The whole house was.

I turned around and then I stopped to run a diagnostic. My joints were stiff, my servos sluggish. Not by much, but enough for me to notice. So I stood and I looked at the window and I flexed a few more joints and calibrated a few other servos and then my diagnostic report came back to say I needed a full service report because of something it called "error 66." I didn't know what that was, but Ada would. That service report was going to have to wait until I got back to the office.

It was night. The window was closed but the blind was open. The world outside was a yellow glow. I watched my own reflection get larger as I walked to the window and then I opened it. I looked out. There were a few guards down on the lawn and the house was lit up brighter than a baseball stadium.

I checked my internal chronometer. I didn't like what it told me so I checked my wristwatch. The two devices were in complete agreement.

"Oi oi!"

I spun around as fast as a robot of my size could spin.

Alfie was standing in the doorway, halfway into his jacket, shirt untucked, tie loose around his neck, hair flapping up like the lid of a trash can. He had a cigarette in his mouth and the light of the lamp on my nightstand flashed in his big glasses.

He paused, arms at angles, shoulders hunched. Then he resumed his journey into his jacket. He cleared his throat.

"Yeah, well, sorry to, ah, disturb, Charlie, but the old man wants to see us, pronto pronto. Got an urgent job, needs doing and needs doing fast, he says."

I checked my chronometer again. I still didn't like what it told me. I checked my wristwatch. Alfie nodded at me then got to work on his tie. "Yeah, well, all work and no play, et cetera, et cetera." He took the cigarette out of his mouth and adjusted his glasses. "Falzarano's study, see you in two shakes."

And then he was gone.

I stood looking at the doorway again. Then I followed. But before I did I checked my internal chronometer and I checked my wristwatch for the third time.

It was eight p.m.

And I had no recollection of the last twelve hours.

28

There was a guard outside Falzarano's study door and as I approached he opened the door for me. I glanced at him as I went in. He seemed tense. I wondered what had happened. Had Ellis come back? Had he been taken back? Captured? Or killed even? Maybe he'd taken a knife to the kidneys or a dive off something very high.

Such things seemed to happen around Zeus Falzarano and a lot could happen in twelve hours.

Twelve hours I had no memory of whatsoever.

The old man was in the study and Alfie was busy adjusting the cuffs of his jacket as he stood in front of the big desk.

I looked past the desk at the rows of shelves stacked with Falzarano's own book. Something about the books made my circuits buzz. I didn't know why.

I snapped out of it when Falzarano pushed himself up

out of his chair and walked around the desk. I had to say he didn't look well. In fact, he looked more than sick. He looked older. *Much* older. And he was leaning on a walking stick, which I hadn't seen before. The stick was black and had a curved silver handle and the shaft was thick and strong. He leaned on it heavily as he walked back around his desk to his chair.

I stood beside Alfie. Alfie watched his boss from behind his glasses, his expression flat.

Falzarano moved with cinematic slowness. He'd been a slick mover back at the restaurant, under the motivation of a surprise machine gun attack, and now that I thought about it I realized that after that night I'd only ever seen him sitting behind his desk in the study. Maybe he was a slow mover. Old people often were. Arthritis and the ravages of time. I was a robot and neither of those things were going to bother me by the time I reached Falzarano's age, which was going to be somewhere in the vicinity of the year two thousand and thirty something.

But tonight every one of Falzarano's years hung heavy on him. He looked at me and Alfie and his face was pale and the cheeks were slack, their weight pulling down on his eyes, showing me two crescents of wet redness beneath them. He was breathing hard.

There was something wrong.

"Ah, Ray, Alfie, my sons, my sons, listen, listen," he said with a voice as light and thin as his skin looked. I moved forward to help him into his chair but the hand that wasn't on the stick waved me off. Alfie didn't move.

"I need you to go and get me a few things," he said as soon as he'd sat down. "A little shopping list, yes, yes?" He leaned back in his leather chair and then he reached forward. His fingertips only just hit the edge of the desk. His notepad was in front of him. He'd written something down but now didn't seem to have the strength even to reach for it.

I pointed. "Here?"

He nodded. I took the ledger. There was an address and a short list of things.

A short list of things that were very surprising.

"Just a few things, yes," said Falzarano. He had his eyes closed now. He lifted a hand. "I trust you and Alfie can handle things."

I looked at the list again. There was nothing about it that I liked. Not the address, not the list.

Certainly not the address.

"Okay," I said. I looked at Alfie. He was still looking at his boss, his lips now pressed together, like someone paying their condolences to the deceased but in desperate need of a cigarette at the graveside. Still he didn't speak.

I frowned on the inside and I pulled the top sheet off the pad and I folded it into quarters and then put the paper into my jacket. I looked down at Falzarano. He was breathing, but it was faint and the skin of his face had gone from pale to virtually translucent. His tie was tight as it always was, held just so by a fine if old-fashioned silver tiepin at the collar.

"Mr. Falzarano?"

His chest moved once, and then was still. He was alive, but clearly sick.

I reached down to loosen his tie. He needed oxygen.

As soon as my fingers touched the silver pin there was a static discharge that made me jerk my hand back. And then

I heard someone swooshing over the carpet toward us.

"I'll take care of him," said Carmina. She marched into the study wearing a heavy embroidered housecoat that covered her top to toe. Her hair was pinned back.

She reached over to Falzarano and was about to do the same thing with his tie as I had been but then she stopped. She looked at me over her shoulder.

"You have the list?"

I nodded.

"Then hurry, please. Quickly! You must waste no time."

She kept looking at me. Then her eyes moved to Alfie. Falzarano made another shuddering breath.

I stood in the corridor.

Alfie sniffed again. "He's in a bad way, eh?"

"Doesn't make much sense," I said. "He was fine before, wasn't he?"

Alfie shrugged. "Who knows. He must be hundred and one bleedin' years old." His hands started a search of his suit for his cigarettes. "So where are we going?"

I took the folded paper out of my jacket. I unfolded it. I read it and I didn't like it any better. I handed it over to Alfie. He stuck an unlit cigarette in his mouth and lifted his glasses off his nose to peer at the paper with his naked eyes.

I don't know if Alfie knew what he was reading, but he whistled all the same and said "blimey" as he handed the paper back.

I read the list again.

It wasn't groceries. It was components. Electronic components that weren't used for building crystal sets or repairing televisions. These were components you built— or *repaired*—computers with.

Computers . . . and robots.

Alfie lit his cigarette and blew smoke into the air. "So you know how to get there?"

I nodded. "Oh yes, I know how to get there, all right."

"Okay, you can drive, then." He held his hand out, indicating I was to lead the way.

I headed to the garage. Alfie followed. As we walked I thought about the missing twelve hours and the buzzing in my circuits was so loud I could hardly hear my processor calculate.

And when I thought about our destination the buzzing did nothing but get an awful lot louder.

Thornton Industrial Electronics and Research.

I was going home.

29

Traffic was good and it took only a half hour to get to Thornton's building in my Buick. All the way there I kept one optic on the telephone that sat between me and Alfie. I wanted to call Ada but I didn't want to talk in front of Alfie. So I just eyed the phone but kept my hands on the wheel.

I pulled up outside the locked gates, and Alfie and I sat there for a minute or so looking at the place. Alfie didn't say anything. He was on the fifth cigarette of the trip and the little pullout ashtray in the dash was reaching its limit. He had his window cracked. The smoke drifted out of it in long blue-gray ribbons.

We were at the right place. The building beyond the gates was dark. About half of the big letters on the front that had once read THORNTON INDUSTRIAL ELECTRONICS AND RESEARCH were still there. The rest had fallen off long ago, leaving nothing but a fading shadow on the pink plasterwork. But you never forget where you were born, even if you were a machine with only twenty-four hours' worth of memory tape inside you.

Time and disuse had not done the building any favors but at least the place was still standing. It was Art Deco like much of the best parts of the city were, a multitiered construction that looked like a wedding cake from the year 2525. The ground beyond the gates were flat concrete and that concrete was cracked in many places, like the plasterwork of the building itself. Weeds grew in the cracks in the lot and in the building itself. The gates were black iron and they had flat silver panels in them that formed the rays of a stylized sun. They looked in better shape than the rest of the place.

I got out of the car. I wanted to leave it just where it was. I wanted a fast getaway. I didn't need to say anything to Alfie. He got out of the car and stood smoking by the gates. He looked at me across the roof of the car and flicked ash into the night air.

"Lovely," he said. "But it doesn't look like the wizard is at home, mate."

"Suits me," I said. I went up to the gates and made short work of the chains that had held them shut for who knew how long. Years, anyway. I didn't wait for Alfie to follow me but he stuck close and when we got to the doors of the main building I made short work of the chains that were holding those doors shut too. Alfie backed up a little and looked straight up at the building.

"Here, Charlie," he said, "looks like this place has been shut up for donkeys. How do we know there's anything left inside?"

I shrugged. "Fair question. Falzarano seems to think there is."

I took the note out from my pocket and offered it to Alfie between two steel fingers. He took a long suck on his cigarette and tossed it onto the cracked concrete, then took the note and unfolded it and seemed to read it while holding his breath. Then he looked up at me.

"You know what this lot is?"

I nodded.

"You know what the old man's going to do with it all?"

I had some ideas about that. Ideas I didn't like. They rattled around in my circuits, bounced between transistors and neuristors and condenser coils like a pinball.

"I might," I said.

I turned back around to the doors and pushed them open. They were stiff with disuse and the wood squealed against the frame.

We went inside.

The lobby of the building was a big rectangular room with a high ceiling. It stretched out ahead of us in a moonlit half-light, ending in two sets of double doors. There was a curved reception desk on our left that matched the curves of the building. On either side of the lobby two big wide staircases climbed up. There was a railed landing above us, like there was back at Falzarano's.

I remembered this place. Somehow I remembered when I'd last seen it. There had been people here. A receptionist in a pink skirt and top. Scientists in white coats.

Somewhere there had been the smell of pipe smoke.

Now it was dark and the place was dusty with the kind of dust you only get inside places that have been closed for years, dust that is thick and slightly sticky. In what moonlight that did come in through the high windows of the building's lobby the whole linoleum floor looked furry.

"Okay," said Alfie. "Okay, lovely." He had his hands in the pockets of his coat and he walked into the middle of the lobby. His footsteps echoed along with his voice. He looked straight up. "So you know where they keep all them doodads, then?"

"I do. The only place this kind of specialized equipment was stored was in the main research laboratory, which is up on the seventh floor."

"Righto," said Alfie. He looked around then headed toward the back of the lobby. Between the two double doors was the elevator. I joined him just as he stabbed the call button with his thumb for the fourth time.

"Dead," he said.

I nodded. "No power. The whole building is dead."

We stood and looked at each other. Alfie pointed to one of the stairs.

"Well, off you go then, Charlie. Lead the way, mate."

I led the way. I knew where I was going.

The stairs were carpeted with thin industrial carpet tiles. They were nothing like the luxurious flooring at Falzarano's, but in the empty building they did a good enough job of muffling our footsteps.

I don't know why I wanted to keep quiet. The building was empty. Had been for years.

But still. I wanted to be quiet.

We arrived on the landing—a mezzanine floor—and I kept going up. Alfie followed behind. He was looking around, his hands still in his pockets. He'd given up smoking. He was on the job now.

The stairwell handrail was dusty. We hit the second floor. The third. Nothing had changed. There was no sound. The dust was thick. Our progress was lit by the moon shining in through the big windows that were all over the place. The light was silver and white and in it everything looked gray.

Seventh floor. The research laboratory.

Thornton's laboratory.

I looked at the ceiling and I looked at the floor and counted the spiders and the cobwebs while I waited for Alfie to arrive. Seven floors was quite a way and while he was faster than me in a straight line he was slower than me when ascending the vertical. When he pulled himself up into the corridor he gave me a nod. I turned and walked on.

We came to a corridor that was completely dark. I heard Alfie's step hesitate behind me. I turned around and turned the light up in my optics a little to shine a path. I saw myself reflected in his big square glasses.

Alfie nodded at me to continue.

The yellow glow from my optics was the best I could do. It wasn't much, but we didn't have far to go. Soon enough I pushed through a set of fire doors and we emerged into a wide corridor that had high windows down one side. The moon was bright outside. It cast long shadows and those shadows made shapes on the floor and the wall in front of us.

I was a robot and even I thought it was creepy. But at least we could see any monsters that might come for us.

I turned my optics back down and we walked a while. The corridor was long and the right side was lined with lots of doors with windows in them. As we passed each one, Alfie took a look through. After the fifth door he stopped. I turned around.

"You sure about this, Charlie?" asked Alfie. "Doesn't look like there's anything left in here at all. Whole place has been cleared out, hasn't it?"

He pointed through the window of the latest door. I joined him and looked inside.

It was a laboratory. The whole floor was full of them. This one was a long room lined with cupboards and benches. There were more long benches running up the middle of the room. Stools were pushed underneath them.

The long benches would have been covered in equipment. Lamps. Magnifying glasses on adjustable arms. Soldering irons. Toolkits. Volt meters. Coils of wire in a dozen gauges. Oscilloscopes and computer banks. The works. The cupboards and drawers that lined the walls would have been filled with more tools and components and spare parts.

There was nothing in the room now. Just the bare benches and a few stools. The cupboards were all closed, but I knew they'd be empty too.

"There's nothing here, Charlie."

"We aren't there yet," I said. "Try to be an optimist."

We walked on and went through two more sets of fire doors and then we arrived.

I stopped in the corridor. I thought I could smell heavy tobacco. I thought I remembered a man with a pipe and glasses and a surprised kind of look leaning out of one of the doors down the corridor.

And then the memories were gone and I wasn't even sure I had really remembered anything.

This was my place of birth. It was bound to stir up all kinds of—

Emotions? No, they weren't emotions, although it was a

little hard to tell. I was programmed to *simulate* emotions. My whole personality was a simulation, a complex organic algorithm taken from a template copied from a real person.

Professor Thornton, my creator.

But that's just what it was—a template. I wasn't him. I didn't think like him. I didn't have his knowledge or experience even if I remembered parts of his life sometimes.

And if I sometimes felt like him then that was just another simulation, my positronic circuits estimating responses based on sensory input and correlating that input with data on my permanent store. Somewhere inside me my logic gates clicked and they clacked and my master program algorithm went up and down and back and forth along an infinite number of pathways and options, at each step comparing the yes-no result with what the template said.

It was a program. *I* was a program. Nothing more. Nothing less.

So I ignored the feeling of weary nostalgia about a place I didn't remember being in before and I ignored the feeling of guilt at something I didn't remember doing.

And I ignored the smell of pipe smoke.

Alfie hadn't said anything. I turned around and jerked my head down the empty corridor.

"Down here," I said.

Alfie adjusted his glasses.

I turned back around and I walked down the corridor toward Thornton's laboratory.

I turned the corner and I stopped. Alfie nearly walked into my back, and he said something I didn't catch because my head was suddenly filled with the sound of crickets on a summer night.

No. Not crickets. Something else. A ticking, loud and fast. And dangerous.

I tuned in and I listened and then I realized what it was I was listening to.

My Geiger counter was racing. If it had been ticking before I hadn't heard it because it usually ticked all the time. Lots of things in the world were radioactive and just like any Joe in the street I didn't need to know about it all. I only needed to know when it was unusual. I would have said dangerous, except radiation didn't bother me much.

But it would bother Alfie. He was still behind me as I took a step backward, forcing him down the corridor.

"What's up, Charlie?"

"Back," I said. "Around the corner."

My Geiger ticked down as we left the corridor and passed through the fire doors. It was still a little high but I figured that in this corridor at least the dose was a little less than what Alfie got from his own cigarettes.

"Wait here," I said. I left Alfie where he was and I stepped back through the fire doors.

The main door to Thornton's lab was dead ahead. The corridor was dark now that the windows were gone so I turned my optics up again.

I didn't like what I saw.

The building itself had been locked up and then chained up. It was shut, closed, out of bounds. The whole place seemed empty. I didn't know who owned it but I guessed it was federal property and they were happy to just let it sink into the foundations of Los Angeles. Seemed a bit of a waste, but it was what it was.

Thornton's research lab was also locked up, but this was different. This explained why they'd left the building intact. They couldn't demolish it. Nor could they move anyone else in.

Because the door to Thornton's lab wasn't just locked, it was sealed. In fact, it wasn't even a door. Where the door had been was a big wide steel plate that had only a very dull sheen under the lights of my optics. The steel plate had a lot of notices posted on it. I read them all, several times. They were mostly notices from the federal government. A warning about trespassing. A warning about being shot. (Who was left to do the shooting?) A warning about tampering and who to call if you saw or heard anything suspicious.

But that wasn't what got my attention. What got my attention was the big diamond-shaped poster right in the middle. It was yellow and had a black symbol on it consisting of a big black dot and three curved fins arcing out from it.

The international symbol for nuclear energy.

I checked my Geiger. It roared like a lion.

Thornton's laboratory was hot.

Of course the items on Falzarano's shopping list were still in the building, because they were all in Thornton's lab. The building had been stripped of everything else of value or interest, but not this part. Nothing could be taken out. Something had happened in there and had left the place a radioactive no-man's-land. All they could do was seal the door and hope for the best.

Radiation didn't bother me, but I didn't want to take anything out of there without precautions. So I turned and went back down the corridor and through the fire doors.

Alfie had lit a cigarette, apparently content that nobody was going to catch us loitering. I saw the end flare in the darkness and I saw his silhouette nod at me.

"What's the story, Charlie?"

I scratched my chin. It made a fingernails-on-blackboard kind of noise and I saw Alfie's shoulders rise up in irritation.

"Sorry," I said. "The lab where the equipment is is hot. Radioactive. I can go in there but taking anything out is going to be a risk."

Alfie nodded and puffed on his cigarette. "So what do we do? Find some kind of lead box to put it in?"

"I don't think we'll find anything here," I said. "You saw the other labs. This whole place had been stripped. But I have another idea."

"Oh yeah?"

"Pass me the list."

Alfie handed me the note. I unfolded it and looked it over. Of course I remembered what it said exactly, but I wanted to be sure. Call it a tic inherited from my creator, the man whose abandoned laboratory was now a sealed tomb.

"Most of these things are small," I said. "They're only components, little things you build into something bigger."

"If you say so, mate."

"Which means I have room."

I tapped my chest. It sounded like someone knocking on a door. Alfie stood there and smoked and stared at me.

"Yeah, well," he said, "I'll take your word for that. You lead-lined or something?"

"No, but the alloy I'm made of is pretty dense. It will do until we get back to Falzarano's."

"And what's the old man going to do? If this gear is as hot as you say it is, he's going to get well burned, ain't he?"

I frowned on the inside. "Unless he's taken precautions." I looked at Alfie. "Maybe that's why he wanted me. He knew I could go in there and get the components."

"Then why bring me along? I'm no good for any of this."

"You can't come in with me, but that's okay," I said. "Go back to the car. It'll be safer there. Drive it up to the main doors and keep it running. When I come back down, we hightail it back to Falzarano's. You drive faster than I do."

Alfie smiled in the dark. "Interesting idea," he said. "And I did fancy a go at your motor."

I nodded at him. "Opportunity knocks. Now go. I'll be down as soon as I can."

Alfie did a mock salute. "Roger that, Charlie," he said, and then he headed away. "Oh," he said, calling back over his shoulder. "Take it easy, won't you?"

And then he was gone and I was alone. I turned and walked back through the fire doors. I faced the steel plate. I wondered what had happened inside Thornton's lab. Some kind of accident? Must have been. With the professor gone, one of his former assistants must have got something very, very wrong.

I turned down my Geiger counter because I didn't need to hear it anymore. I had to go in, and there was no point worrying about it.

And with the Geiger counter off, I finally heard another sound. I had no idea how long it had been going on, but Alfie hadn't said anything, so it must have been new.

I looked at the steel plate.

From somewhere behind it, a telephone rang.

I had a feeling I knew who was calling.

30

The steel plate over the laboratory door was made to keep people out, but whoever had sealed the joint hadn't counted on a robot being interested in getting behind it. I made short work of it, getting a good grip on the edge and yanking it toward me. It didn't take much. The steel plate had been bolted onto the wooden frame of the lab door behind it, so a couple of hefty tugs and the whole thing came away, wood and all, from the wall. I waited a moment for the brick dust to settle and then I placed the plate against the wall to my right and took a step across the threshold.

It was dark beyond the door so I kept my optics high. I moved in I saw that what windows there had been were covered with more steel plates.

The lab was intact, the whole place left like a museum.

Or a mausoleum.

Equipment was stacked everywhere, big boxy machines

and computers as tall as refrigerators with as many miles of magnetic tape strung around their reels as there was back at my own office in Hollywood. There were stools with short backs all around the benches and some of them even had white lab coats draped over the back of them, and some of the benches had screwdrivers and soldering irons and needle-nosed pliers scattered like abandoned toys over blueprints and worksheets and clipboards. Whatever had happened had happened fast and everyone had got the hell out before it was too late.

The fully equipped robotics laboratory included a telephone on the wall next to the main door. The telephone was red and it looked important and it was still ringing as I stood there.

I lifted the handset to the side of my head.

"Ada, I'd love to talk, really I would, and I've got a hell of a story to tell, but this place is a little warmer than I'd normally like it and I don't want to hang around."

Ada laughed inside my head. "Just what is it with you and radiation?"

"You'll have to tell me."

"Maybe I will one day," said Ada. "So, how does it feel to be back home?"

I looked around the lab. I looked at all the equipment. At the far end of the room was a robot-shaped alcove like the one back in my office. I looked at that and then I found I couldn't shift my optics from its direction. I felt a pang of something then. Those diodes down my left side. They flashed, all at once. I frowned on the inside as I held the phone to my head and I thought maybe it would be nice to remember things once in a while.

Like where you came from.

I decided to ignore Ada's question. I checked the radiation count again and I didn't like what I found.

"Listen, I've got an error 66," I said, "and I've lost twelve hours of memory time. Now I'm in Thornton's lab looking for old components. I don't like any of that and I have a feeling they're all connected somehow. Are they?"

Ada hummed inside my head. "Error 66?"

"Error 66. Ideas?"

She hummed again. "Let me look it up. What's Falzarano got you looking for?"

I ran off the list of components. When I was done Ada gave a whistle over the rim of her coffee mug. "You've come to the right place, then," she said.

"Is it my memory tape? Is error 66 something to do with a twelve-hour record failure?"

Ada finished her nonexistent cigarette and I could have sworn I heard her stub out the remnants in an ashtray made of orange carnival glass.

"I said I'd look it up, Ray. Don't worry about it. We'll run a service report when you get back. You're made of solid stuff, chief. It won't be anything important."

"Easy for you to say."

"Do you trust me, Ray?"

I said I did but there was a pause before I did it. I didn't know where that pause came from but it was there all the same. If Ada noticed she didn't mention anything.

"Okay, listen hard, detective. I've done a little digging and there's some information you need."

I managed to refocus on the rest of the laboratory that wasn't the alcove. I wanted to see the components for

Falzarano or at least see where I should be looking while Ada yakked in my ear.

"You get a hit on Coke Patterson?" I asked.

"Forget about Coke Patterson," said Ada. "I'm talking about your friends Alfie Micklewhite and the lovely Carmina."

"Okay."

"They're not who they say they are."

"Why doesn't that surprise me?"

"No, listen Ray, I want you to pay attention here."

"I am paying attention but make it sharp."

"Cut it with the countdown and listen good, Ray."

I sighed. Alfie would have got the car up to the building by now and would be waiting while I let a good dose of radiation out into the air of Los Angeles.

"You have my undivided attention," I said.

"Which is exactly what you need to avoid from your two friends."

"Alfie and Carmina?"

"Alfie and Carmina do not exist," said Ada. "Alfie's real name is Francis Cane, and Carmina is Professor Carmen Blanco, late of a Colombian research institute that was a state secret right up until it got blown up in the little civil war they have bubbling away down there."

"Late?"

"She went up with the building, Ray. Five years ago."

"She's looking good for it. And who's Francis Cane? Alfie told me he was a gangster from London."

"Oh, he's from London all right. Only he's not a gangster. He's a private contractor."

"For?"

"A company called International Automatic."

"Okay," I said. I thought about the name. Nothing came to mind. "And?"

"And nothing," said Ada. "All you need to do is stay away from Francis Cane and Carmen Blanco. You got that, chief?"

"Easier said than done. Alfie is waiting for me in the car and Carmina has the run of the house, if she isn't actually *running* it already. Falzarano's sick and she's stepped in to take over."

"Okay, do your best, Ray. Just wait it out until we get the word."

I sighed like a dying air conditioner shuddering its last. "Our illustrious client is taking their sweet time about it. What else do they think I'm going to dig up?"

"Well, finish Falzarano's shopping and then see what happens, okay, chief?"

There was something I didn't like about how this conversation was playing out. Ada sounded . . . not annoyed exactly. But there was a pointedness to her tone that was unfamiliar.

And unsettling. Like the job. I was supposed to kill Falzarano but only when I was told to. And in the meantime I was keeping company with two people who Ada had just told me to keep away from while my system was throwing an error 66 and twelve hours was missing from my memory tape.

Unsettling was one way of describing it, that was for sure.

I switched the telephone to the other side of my head.

"This doesn't feel right, Ada."

"Yeah, well, life gives you lemons, you make lemonade."

"Why do I get the feeling you're not telling me something?"

"Chief, there's a lot I tell you and a lot I don't and not all of it you remember, remember?"

"Something doesn't add up. Who's the client?"

Ada didn't say a thing.

"Who's the client, Ada?" I asked again. "Do you know?"

"You need to hurry back to Falzarano," she said.

I looked around the laboratory. I looked at all the equipment. I ran the list of components I was supposed to collect through my code parse compiler.

"What was the late Carmen Blanco a professor of, exactly?"

Ada said nothing.

"It was robotics, wasn't it? Ada, what aren't you telling me?"

"Just trust me, Ray? Okay? There's not long to go now."

And then the phone went dead and I was left holding it in the radioactive laboratory of my creator.

31

I was back downstairs with the goods in another five minutes. Alfie didn't say anything when I got into the car, he just gunned the engine and we took off. He drove with two hands on the wheel and his elbows locked. He drove fast, like a race car driver, his chin tucked into his chest, his eyes fixed on the road ahead. The cigarette was gone, as was the ever-present curl of his lip as he mused on a private joke.

I watched him a little while. Alfie Micklewhite, also known as Francis Cane. I wondered if Falzarano knew his real name. Probably not and he probably didn't know his lady Carmina was Carmen Blanco, a deceased robotics professor from a secret lab in Colombia that had very conveniently been reduced to rubble with her still inside it.

Supposedly.

The Buick was big and heavy, an inelegant thing built for a specific purpose, to carry a very heavy robot around town as he went about his private detecting business. It had customized shock absorbers and transmission, customized steering, customized engine. Under my steel and titanium hands it was perfectly fine in the same way that riding an elephant through an Asian jungle was perfectly fine.

But under Alfie's hands the car sang. After the initial slow acceleration and lurching deceleration he seemed to understand the engine, and after the first two tiling curves of the road he seemed to understand the machine as a whole.

All of which is to say he was a good driver and we made excellent time.

Thornton Industrial was in Pasadena, a ways north of Los Angeles proper. Falzarano's castle was buried in a canyon to the west. Alfie's route of choice was the most direct, which meant winding the car up one hill and down another with nothing but the wind rushing around us and the night sky spinning high above.

"We all right, Charlie?" asked Alfie, never once taking his focus off piloting my big and heavy car along narrow and winding roads.

"We are," I said. The components from the lab were inside my chest, pressed against my memory tape, the curve of the new panel providing ample room. I checked a few readings. My Geiger counter was having a hell of a time trying to work out why I was radioactive on the inside but not on the outside, so I turned it off. The leak of atomic energy through my chassis was slow but sure, but we'd be fine so long as we got to Falzarano's place soon. Which, with the way Alfie threw the car around the hills, we would.

"You're not cooking me liver or anything, sitting there?"

I glanced at Alfie. "No, there's no radiation leakage." That wasn't quite the whole truth. "You're perfectly safe, but all the same, we should get this stuff back to Falzarano as soon as we can." That was a little more accurate.

Alfie nodded and if anything he pushed his foot farther toward the floor and pushed the car faster along the road. The headlights swept this way and that as we drove up the side of a valley. Falzarano's was not far. There was no other traffic.

Then Alfie unwrapped one hand from the wheel and dived it inside his jacket. I watched as he pulled out his packet of cigarettes and, without giving it any thought at all, extracted a new one with his teeth. Packet returned to his jacket, he began fishing around for his lighter.

"Here," I said and I reached over, holding two fingers a hair apart. I shorted the solenoid and the inside of the car was lit by a blue spark.

Alfie made a clicking noise with his tongue which I took to be his way of saying thanks. Then he cracked his window about an inch to let the smoke out.

That's when I heard it. Alfie's attention was back on driving and he wasn't slowing down. But there was another noise from outside.

I turned in my seat and wrapped an arm around the back of Alfie's so I could really get a good look out the rear windshield. The road was lit red by our taillights and the tarmac was moving under us at a good pace.

Then I saw a glint. Nothing more. Then it was gone. Then it glinted again.

We reached the crest of the hill and began to spiral down it. I glanced at Alfie.

"Kill the engine."

"What?"

I turned back around to look out the rear. "I said kill the engine. Let it coast for a moment."

"If you say so, Charlie." Alfie twisted the key and the motor died. We glided on down the hill under the power of gravity.

Then Alfie stiffened in his seat. He squinted into his wing mirror.

"Oi, we're being followed."

I nodded. "We are. They've got their lights off."

Alfie gave the Buick a rolling start and then gunned the engine. I turned back around.

Alfie looked at me and I looked at him.

"Lose them," I said.

"No sooner said than done, mate," said Alfie. He pulled the gear stick and pressed the accelerator and the engine roared and the Buick kicked up on its rear wheels and we scrambled down the hill.

Somewhere behind us the headlights of our tail flicked on. They knew they'd been made and now they were going to try to catch up.

Alfie threw the wheel to the left and we crossed the centerline to get a better run down the hill. It was late and the road was empty and for that I was thankful.

I checked my wing mirror. The lights of the car following us loomed brightly and were getting brighter.

"They're gaining," I said.

"Well yeah, that's because they're faster than we are. I mean, I like your car, Charlie, but it's not going to win at Monte bloody Carlo, now is it?"

I pursed my lips on the inside. The lights behind us got bigger and bigger and then they were on us.

And then the Buick kicked again, but this time it wasn't Alfie's driving. The car behind nudged us, nose to tail. I turned around again and saw the headlights recede then suddenly loom again and our car was rocked for the second time as the tail rammed us.

"They're trying to force us off the road," said Alfie. "Bloody hooligans." He checked the mirror, then he hissed and turned around in his seat to check out the rearview himself.

"Eyes on the road, Alfie!"

"It's the same bloody car!"

I turned and looked too but the car had backed off, a cat preparing itself for another pounce.

"What car?"

Alfie wrenched the gearshift and returned his focus to the darkness ahead. "The one the other night, the one we nearly ran into. Wasn't far from here, either."

I didn't remember anything about any near miss, but there was nothing too unusual about that so I was prepared to take Alfie's word for it. I pointed through the windshield, somewhat unnecessarily.

"Okay, so let's shake them, Alfie," I said. "Come on, you said you liked to drive cars fast, so show me what you got."

Alfie didn't answer but he did smile. With one arm locked on the wheel, his other fell to the parking brake down by his seat.

The road opened out as another came off it, the intersection forming a big oval and that oval was lit by a yellow sodium lamp. I checked behind and saw the other car materialize into corporeal existence as it came under the harsh lighting.

The car was black or near to it, sleek and brand new.

There were two people in it. I couldn't see them well but they looked like they were wearing hats. The driver was hunched over the wheel. The front bumper of the car was chromed and it had a nasty dent across the front.

"Hold onto something," said Alfie. I grabbed a hold of the handle above my door and wished us the best of luck as Alfie accelerated into the intersection, then spun the wheel and yanked the handbrake. The car traveled horizontally, tires screaming, the intersection filling with a great cloud of acrid smoke. Alfie wrenched the wheel in toward the opposite lock and the car bucked and threatened to roll. Then he straightened up and floored it and I discovered we were traveling back in the direction we had come.

Toward the other car. Alfie had said we'd nearly hit that very same car the other night. It didn't look like we were going to miss a second time.

My grip tightened on the handle. If we crashed, I'd be fine. The car, not so much. Alfie, certainly not.

I hoped he knew what he was doing.

The whole thing took three seconds. I saw our headlights travel up the hood of the black car. I saw the passenger draw one arm up over his face as he recoiled. I saw the driver staring wide-eyed and worried.

Alfie pressed the accelerator and he did something else too.

He laughed.

And then the black car swerved, but not fast enough. We were heavy, an unstoppable force. The black car was far from immoveable. It turned to our right and shot off toward the edge of the road as the Buick clipped the rear end. The bang was like a gunshot and something long and chrome came at us at an angle and cracked against the windshield. The glass held and the chrome piece slid off our hood as we blasted down the hill.

I looked in the rearview just in time to see the taillights of the other car lift up way too high and then vanish as the car went over the side of the road. The hills here were steep and it was a long way down to the bottom.

I didn't want to estimate the survival chances of the driver and his passenger.

I turned back around. Alfie laughed and we drove down and down and down.

I'd been wrong about the windshield. Right in the center of my vision there was a chip about the size of a pea, a tiny white star in a field of black.

"We'll put in some miles, Charlie," said Alfie. "Then we'll go back around to Falzarano's the long way, okay? Anyone who was following the car what was following us won't be able to find us and they'll be too busy getting their friends out of the wreck. It'll put us behind schedule though."

I nodded. "I think this counts as extenuating circumstances. We got what Falzarano wants and Falzarano will just have to like it."

Alfie nodded and laughed, and then he glanced down between his legs.

"Oh, bloody hell."

"What is it?"

"Dropped me cigarette in all the commotion." He looked at me. He didn't look happy. "I've only gone and burned a hole in me bleeding trousers."

I smiled on the inside and then I laughed. It made a sound not dissimilar to the sound the gearbox made when

Alfie pulled the handbrake turn.

Alfie glanced at me and the road and me again. And then his face cracked into a grin and then he laughed too. He wound his window down and his blond curls blew around his face.

I helped Alfie laugh but wondered all the while why Ada wanted me to stay away from Francis Cane.

We laughed all the way to Falzarano's castle, and there the laughter stopped.

32

We were met at the house by Falzarano's boys. Lots of them, along with lots of rifles and mean looks and dogs that barked and snapped and spit. The big garage was open and Alfie raced toward the empty spot that was waiting for us only to slam the brakes on as one of Falzarano's guards stood right in our way with a hand up. With the Buick stationary and only half in the bay, the guard jerked a thumb back up at the house.

I reached for my door handle only to find the door being opened by another guard. I glanced at Alfie and saw that his door was open too. He gave me a look and pulled his cigarette pack out of his jacket pocket.

I got out. The guard by my door nodded back toward the house. I looked around. All the guards were looking at us—the guards at the house, the guards at the garage, the guards lining the driveway all the way from the big gates and stone lions at the top down to the ornamental fountain at the bottom.

And all spooked in equal measure. More than before. Something was up. Maybe they'd found Ellis?

Or—

"What's happened?" I asked. "Is Mr. Falzarano okay?"

"Inside, and sharp," said my guard. He grabbed my arm like he meant it and he squeezed just as hard.

My escort and I hustled around to the steps but I pulled up and glanced behind me. Alfie—Francis Cane—was in conference with the guard by the car. He saw me looking and waved at me.

"Go on," he said. "I'll see what the fuss is. Get that stuff to the old man, quick!"

I nodded and trotted up the steps and then went through the front door and walked across the checkerboard of the entrance hall. The hall was lined with guards and there were more on the stairs and up on the landing above me.

"Ray!"

Carmina came out of the long passageway. She was wearing one of her trademark split dresses but most of it was hidden under a long white coat made of a stiff and heavy fabric. A lab coat, not entirely unlike the ones left to rot back at Thornton's laboratory.

Just like the ones a professor might wear when they were on the job.

Carmina—Carmen Blanco—was moving as fast as my guard had been.

"What's with the circus?" I asked.

Carmina's brow creased into a V shape and she shook her head. "Circus? Ah, circus. The men, they have heard about their leader. Word spreads more quickly than fire."

"What's happened to him?"

She ignored me. "What took you so long?" she asked. She took my arm much like the guard did and together we migrated down the long passageway toward Falzarano's study. I thought about Ada's warning about Professor Carmen Blanco and how I was supposed to keep her at a little more than an arm's length.

"We had a little trouble on the way back from the laboratory," I said as we sailed through the carpet.

"Trouble?"

I nodded. "We were followed. Two guys, black car. No idea who they were. Alfie thought he'd seen the car before but they were pretty keen on running us off the road."

Carmina stopped where she was. I took a few more steps before realizing I was out on my own. I stopped and turned back around. Carmina was sinking into the carpet and her expression wasn't a happy one.

"What happened to them?"

"We ran them off the road first."

Carmina wrung her hands together. She looked pretty worried. I wondered if she'd seen the car before, too. Like Alfie—the other person in this building who was using another name.

It occurred to me that one of the uses for a false name was to hide yourself away. Particularly if the world thought you had died in your laboratory during a civil war. Falzarano had taken in Emerson Ellis for his own protection—albeit against the businessman's will.

Was Falzarano hiding Professor Carmen Blanco here too? Only, unlike Ellis, it didn't seem to be against her will.

Anything but. Falzarano was building a factory. A *robot* factory. He had the land, he had the plans, he had all the experts—the late Vaughan Delaney, the missing Emerson Ellis. The not-dead Professor Carmen Blanco. The parts I'd grabbed from Thornton's lab, they weren't for Falzarano. He was an old man, the last of his generation of mobsters, an émigré from the old world whose star had risen long before the great robot revolution of the 1950s.

Carmina was the roboticist. She would know exactly what to do with the parts. Quite what that was, I still didn't know.

Maybe the guys in the car had. That same car had been in the hills before. Then they'd tailed Alfie and me from Thornton's lab. More than tailed—they'd wanted to stop us from getting back to Falzarano's. They'd wanted to stop us making the delivery to Carmina.

They knew she was here. And if Falzarano was hiding her, then that meant word had leaked out from within his little family.

My logic gates flipped and clacked and somewhere deep inside a light came on.

Because there was someone else in this building who wasn't who he said he was.

Alfie Micklewhite. Francis Cane, according to his mother.

Was he the mole? He wasn't hiding. Falzarano had hired him. Like he'd hired me. Which meant Falzarano didn't know his real name. And there was more than a fair chance he didn't know that Alfie was already employed, but by someone else—an outfit called International Automatics. I didn't know who they were or what kind of company that was, but from the name alone I think I could make a fairly wild guess.

Robotics.

But their angle, I didn't get. They must have known Falzarano was up to something that fell within an overlapping field of interest. I could believe them sending in one of their own, infiltrating Falzarano's organization to find out just what that something was. Once embedded, the man from IA finds out that the old man's amour is a roboticist the world thought was dead. That information is fed back to his masters, they send more agents in to—

To what? Capture her? Kill her? Or kill Falzarano?

It would take more than a couple of guys in a car to do that. And if my pal Alfie was the leak then that meant the bit on the road was just a bit of dangerous theater for the benefit of nobody but me.

Something wasn't adding up. But the programming I had as a private detective told me I was getting close.

I lifted my hat from my head and used it to point down to the doors to Falzarano's study.

"I don't know what's going on here," I said—truer words had not been synthesized—"but I get the feeling there's more than a little urgency to the matter, so shall we?"

Carmina nodded and walked toward the doors. I followed her. Then she stopped and turned around. The doors remained closed.

"I'll take them from here," she said. "Do you have them?"

There was a hint of fear in her voice, like after all this I didn't have what she wanted after all. "Where are they?" Her words tumbled out.

I took a step back and undid my coat. Then I undid my

jacket. My shirt was already unbuttoned from when I'd been back at Thornton's. I pushed my tie over one shoulder.

When I had enough room I thought about undoing the locks on my chest unit.

And then I paused.

"I've got them," I said, and Carmina's hands moved up to touch me. It might have been an involuntary movement, the way her eyes got wide at the same time. "The components are all here but they're hot."

"Hot?" Her hands dropped away. Her brow creased.

"Radioactive," I said. "Not a lot, but enough. You'll need protective gear. Maybe a lead-lined box if you have one."

Carmina shook her head. "There is no time. I will be fine. I will not be exposed for very long."

"What about the old man?" I nodded toward the doors. "Either he's in there wearing a radiation suit or there's something you're not telling me. I don't know why he wanted me to go and get these components but I have the strangest feeling you know exactly what they're for, don't you?"

Carmina flinched like someone had slapped her. She looked at me with narrowed eyes.

"Don't be a fool," she said. "Of course I know what they are. Who do you think wrote out the list?"

"So what do you want them for? The way I see it, there are only two things these components are good for. One is building a computer. The other is repairing a computer. The old man must have quite a calculator locked away in that big desk of his."

Carmina sighed and waved her hand at me. "There is no time for this now! Please, give me the components. You can see Mr. Falzarano later."

"Or a robot. Because that's what a robot is. A computer, just one that can move around and wear a hat."

I watched her for a moment. She stood with her head level to my chest unit. Then she snapped her fingers. "There is no time for this. Give them to me, quickly."

I sighed. It sounded like the brakes failing on an eighteen-wheeler.

Then I unlocked my chest unit. It opened. I reached in and took out the three components I'd taken from the lab.

"Neutron-flow reversal coil, gamma combine array, triode condenser." I handed them over.

Carmina took the objects in both hands. She held them gingerly, but I guessed they were a little warm from being inside my chest. The radiation she wouldn't be able to feel. Not immediately.

I turned my Geiger counter up and I counted the ticks as the hallway was slowly flooded with atomic energy like a ship that had just struck an iceberg.

"Don't hold onto them too long," I said. "And when you're done you might want a trip to the hospital. I'm sure one of Falzarano's boys will be happy to help out."

Carmina's jaw snapped shut with an audible click. "I told you, I know what I'm doing."

I believed her.

And then she opened the door to the study and went through. The doors closed and I was alone in the corridor. I stood there calculating in my loafers and then headed back the way I had come. I had a few questions for Alfie, and I was determined to get them.

And I was just as determined to find out exactly what it was that Ada wasn't telling me.

That was when the sound came again. A deep hum, the sound of a generator straining, the lights in the corridor dimming in sympathy before going back to full brightness.

And then a moment later it happened again. I turned my Geiger counter back on and listened to it tick away. I checked the reading twice.

It was lower than it should have been. The doors to Falzarano's study were not lead-lined and the room beyond should have been warming up.

It wasn't.

I headed to the doors. I opened them. I stood in the doorway. I looked around.

The office was how I remembered it. The piano was there along with all the books, the easy chairs, the big desk.

Carmina wasn't. Neither was Falzarano.

The room was empty.

33

Falzarano's office was a dead end. The room was buried at the center of his country pile and there were no windows. There was only one door and right now I was standing under the frame. Yet the fact remained that Carmina was not present. Nor her boss, Zeus Falzarano.

No, not her boss. Her *patron*, the old mobster funding the continuation of her robotics research after secretly extracting her from Colombia under the cover of a conveniently placed civil war.

I did a circuit of the shelves. There were a lot of books and I wondered if anybody ever read them or if they had whether they would ever read them again. If a book was a souvenir of a journey, there were a lot of postcards in this room.

Including Falzarano's own magnum opus. A whole case of them, wall to wall, floor to ceiling, in pride of place behind the desk.

Except it wasn't a bookcase. It was a door. A buzzing in my circuits told me I already knew that, but when I queried my data tape a subroutine threw me an error 66.

Error 66 stung like all hell. I stumbled as my master program slipped its clutch, my positronic central processor trying very hard to keep me away from an emergency system restart. That explained the twelve-hour gap on my tape. Whatever error 66 was, it had caused an emergency restart before. Several times in fact. As the office bucked like a bronco in front of my optics, my diagnostic subroutine very kindly showed me the system log, as if to say I told you so.

Ten program breaks, ten errors 66, ten restarts.

I fell against the piano, arm wheeling for purchase while I regained control of my system after the ill-advised query. I made a note to myself not to do that again. After three seconds I felt normal enough to adjust my hat and tie. I used my reflection in the glossy surface of the piano to help. Someone sure looked after the thing. I supposed that someone was Carmina. I hadn't heard her play it in a while but I guessed she was a little too preoccupied now, having gone back to her old job with the lab coat.

Then I noticed a curious fact. The lid that hid the keyboard had been left open. I had knocked the ivories with my hand when I'd gotten dizzy. I didn't really know anything about the anatomy of the thing. I wasn't musical, which I guessed meant Thornton hadn't been musical either.

Neither was the piano, because the keys hadn't made a sound.

I frowned and pressed the keys again. Now I could hear the dull thudding sound they made and I could feel the vibration of the hammers inside the piano hitting something.

If it was the strings they were being muted. I looked down at the pedals but there were three of them and none of them gave any indication of what they might do.

I tried more keys with more fingers. Nothing at all. Which was mildly interesting in that the piano had been working before and it wasn't working now and that had nothing to do with my spell of electronic vertigo.

Another fact about the piano was that it was big, a grand of the concert variety, and must have posed a few problems of a logistical nature during installation. It was less an instrument, more a piece of furniture. One with a lid and a big space inside.

A pretty good place to hide something of a not insignificant size.

I lifted the top of the piano. I held it at an arm's height and I stood there and thought long and hard about what I found underneath.

Someone had had the same idea as I had.

There was a body inside. It was lying face down, diagonally across the strings. It was a tight fit but fit he did.

I didn't need to turn him over to see who it was. I recognized the round head and the halo of brown hair that curved around the sides.

Emerson Ellis, late of Ellis Building and Construction. Last seen drowning his sorrows in Falzarano's expensive scotch and presumed to have reached freedom after shimmying down the trellis outside his room. Assumed to be guilty of the unlikely killing of one of Falzarano's boys.

He'd escaped, all right. But just not in the way he had anticipated, I'm sure.

I glanced around the body. There was no sign of injury,

although I would have to turn him over to make sure. But there didn't seem to be any blood in the piano.

I lowered the lid. I looked at the piano and I looked at my reflection in the lid.

The piano was a good place to hide the body only if the piano was never played. But it was played, by Carmina. She'd make the discovery soon enough, although she was a little busy with Falzarano for the moment.

Unless she was the one who had killed him. She was the only one who touched the piano, as far as I knew. Maybe she'd used it as a hiding place knowing that nobody else would touch the damn thing. It was a good spot until she could find a better one.

Except she would have needed help to get him into the instrument. And to get him out. One of Falzarano's boys perhaps. Falzarano was her patron, but in her time in exile from Colombia, hidden in Falzarano's Hollywood castle, Carmina had wrangled power away from the old man. Falzarano's boys would do anything she told them to do.

Would that include staging his room, breaking the trellis? Perhaps. But killing one of their own kind?

That I was less sure of.

I pulled myself away from the piano and sailed across the rug to Falzarano's desk. I walked around it and I considered the wall of books that hid a door. I turned my Geiger counter up to maximum. My head was filled with the pink and white and brown noise and as I stood there and scanned the wall I listened to the pops and crackles and snaps that broke out from the rush of sound. Then I looked around the rest of the room, just quickly, just to be sure. I was. Because when I looked back at the shelves in front of me they popped and crackled a whole lot more than the rest of the room.

I pulled one of the books off the shelf. Behind the book was more wood. I pulled off another copy. And then another. And then another. And then I kept going until Falzarano's masterpiece was scattered all over the floor around his desk and the shelves were three-quarters empty. It wasn't until I got to the end of the fourth row down that I found it.

A button. Easy to find if you knew where to look. I pressed it and there was a click and the bookshelf moved, swinging out away from me on a silent and well-oiled hinge. It moved about an inch and then stopped right where it was.

I didn't need another invitation. I pushed the bookcase open like the door it really was. Beyond was another passageway. More thick carpet. More wood paneling. More gold light fittings with pink shades.

And a sound. Sounds, plural. A hum not unlike the sound of something using a high voltage. A whirring sound that was rhythmic, a pattern repeated. Just like the clicking of something switching in sequence, automatically.

These sounds were coming from the door at the end of the new passage. And they were all familiar to me. They were the sounds of reel-to-reel tapes spinning, of microswitches flipping, of hot electronics humming.

The sound of the computer room back at my office. The sound of Ada.

And underneath it all, the buzzing of my own circuits, telling me what I already knew.

That I'd been here before.

I stepped up to the door, and I opened it, and I went inside.

34

The walls and floor were white. The ceiling was a darker blue. The room was roughly square and up against the walls were computer banks and mainframes and consoles with keyboards and buttons and switches and levers, and what space wasn't given over to controls you could touch was covered in lights you could read, lights that flashed in sequence, lights that flashed at random, and lights that stayed lit. There were reel-to-reel tapes that spun around and around. The room buzzed and hummed and ticked and burbled like the computer room back in my office. That was because that's just what it was—a computer room, almost identical to Ada's, right down to the alcove in the wall across from me.

Alcoves. This computer room had more than one. There were three, side-by-side. Two were occupied.

Only not by robots.

I stepped closer.

In the first alcove on my left was a young man with oiled hair slicked back from a clean-shaven face that was square-jawed and heavy-browed. He wore a dark suit and his tie was narrow. He had sunglasses on his face, just like the rest of Falzarano's boys, but unlike the others I knew this one's name.

It was Stefano, and when I'd last seen him—according to Ada's pickup—he'd been shot at virtually point-blank range by Alfie Micklewhite as the three of us had stood in front of Falzarano's desk. Stefano still wasn't breathing as his body leaned back at a small angle in the alcove, but his suit was new and free of bullet holes. I had half a mind to check his torso for wounds, but I was a little distracted by the occupant of the third alcove along on my right.

That occupant being Zeus Falzarano.

Like his deceased former employee, Falzarano lay back at a small angle. His arms were by his side. His mouth was closed, as were his eyes. And like Stefano, he wasn't breathing, but I had a feeling he didn't need to. Because from between the buttons of the shirt over his chest extended a fat cable, a thing of soft corrugated gray plastic that snaked out of him and into the console beside the alcove.

I recognized that kind of cable. It was the same as the one I was attached to each and every time I went to the office and settled in for the night.

Zeus Falzarano. Sicilian import, career criminal, master of his domain, former kingpin of the West Coast. A man who looked younger than he was, according to some. A man who had locked himself away from the eyes of the world. A man who wanted to build a robotics factory and who was hiding a roboticist to help him.

A man who was old and vital, until he was suddenly old and weak. A man who had retired from his perpetual position behind his big desk and had slipped into something a little less comfortable than the big leather chair. A man with a cable plugged into his chest just like a—

I stood there and felt the voltage tick up in a modular somewhere in the back of my head. As I looked at Falzarano's face I reached around under my jacket with one hand and I pulled at my shirt and ran my steel-titanium fingertips over the seams that crisscrossed the small of my back where my batteries were housed. The seal was still tight and I counted as many rivets as I could reach with one hand and then I felt it.

The alloy I was made out of was hardly indestructible but difficult to scratch. I had a noticeable mark on my cheek from something I had no memory of and after the little adventure down at the Bacchanalian I figured my chest plate could probably have done with a polish, but other than that I was factory-fresh.

All except for the line I could feel on my back plate. I couldn't very well see it but I could feel it. It was nothing, a hairline an inch long, running at an angle from a seam to a rivet.

The mark left by someone trying to get the panel off without the proper tools.

I withdrew the hand and I tucked my shirt into my pants and I looked at Falzarano and then I looked at the computer room. Sure, there were tools here, but this was a computer room, not a laboratory and certainly not a factory. No, the factory would come later, along with the industrial equipment needed to open up a robot like myself.

But that hadn't stopped somebody trying. I stopped looking around the room because I knew I had seen it before. I'd been in here. I might even have been in one of the alcoves, perhaps facing the wrong way while someone tried and failed to crack my shell.

I looked at Falzarano. Then I looked at Stefano. The boss, perhaps I could understand. He had a cable coming out of his chest. That was a clue at the very least. But the dead gunman lying in the other space posed more of a question.

I leaned in. He was dead, of that I had no doubt. His skin was pale and when I rested the back of a finger on his cheek I could feel it was cold too.

And then I saw it. This close and Stefano's secret was revealed.

I stepped back and reached forward and took Stefano's sunglasses by one corner and pulled. The sunglasses stayed just where they were and I pulled some more and I could feel the resistance, something elastic, something that felt like it would break if I pulled any harder.

Which is exactly what I did. There was a click, and the glasses came away, but not very far. I stepped back in and took in the view from a side angle.

The back of the sunglasses were nothing but a nest of wires, a cat's cradle of filaments that stretched out from Stefano's empty eye sockets.

That explained why Falzarano's boys—some of them, anyway—wore their glasses all the time, even at night, on account of the fact that they couldn't take the things off. They weren't glasses, they weren't even eyes—they were *optics*.

"Oi, Charlie, hello?"

Alfie.

I turned at the voice, but Falzarano and Stefano were still alone in the computer room. Alfie called out again. He was out in Falzarano's office. I'd left the bookcase door open.

I slid Stefano's glasses back into place and motored out of the computer room, closing the double doors behind me. I headed down the passageway and met Alfie just as he stepped through the door.

"Stone me!" he said. "What's all this, then? Secret passages and priest holes, eh? I tell you, the old man gets ten out of ten for authenticity, eh, Charlie?"

I ignored the question and ushered him back into the office. Alfie tripped on some of the books scattered around the big desk but by the time he'd righted himself I had the bookcase closed behind me.

"What is it?" I asked.

"Here, look. Bloody balloon's gone up and all."

I processed this and came up with nothing.

"English, please. American vernacular if you have it."

"Outside," he said. "There's a right old fuss. There's cars up at the road, all over the show. The boys have seen people, down in the woods, too, like they're trying to sneak in. It's a right old doo-lally. I've been looking for you all over. All hands on deck, mate, all hands on deck! So pull your finger out and get a bloomin' move on!"

Alfie rushed off and left a trail of blue cigarette smoke in his wake.

And then the telephone on Falzarano's desk rang. I picked it up. I knew it was for me.

"What's going on, Ada?"

"Didn't your mother teach you to say 'hello' first?"

"I've found out Falzarano's secret."

"Do tell."

I told her. I described the computer room. I described the alcoves and people who were in those alcoves. When I was done Ada sipped her coffee for a moment or two and then she spoke.

"Good boy, Ray. Very good. Now, listen. I've got some instructions for you."

I frowned on the inside and somewhere in my circuits Ada stirred more creamer into her cup.

"No comment on Falzarano and the fact that he's not entirely what he looks like on the outside? Or that his boys are perhaps even further in that general direction? Or did you already know?"

"No, I didn't know, but now I do. You've done good. The client is going to be very pleased."

"You think this is what they wanted, along with the blueprints?"

"I'd put money on it, chief. But there's a time and a place for this conversation, and pretty soon you're going to be out of both of them. You've got company coming, and lots of it."

I glanced out of the open doors of the office. Alfie was long gone and I couldn't see or hear anyone else.

"So I heard," I said. "Who are they? You want me to get out?"

"As fast as your little legs will take you. But not before you've done the job."

"I'm not sure I like the timing, Ada. But I think I can handle Falzarano."

"That's great, but the job's changed."

"What do you want me to do?"

Ada sipped her coffee. "I want you to kill everyone, Ray."

There was a pause and a beat and I listened to the ticking of the fast hand of a stopwatch far away.

"Nobody gets out of this alive."

35

Alfie had been right. Falzarano's castle was in uproar. I hit the entrance hall and kept on going to the main door, but on my way across the checkerboard I had to stop to let a group of boys with guns rush out from somewhere deeper in the house. By the time I'd followed, the group had already split around the fountain and were racing up the drive in the night, rifles clacking and gravel crunching and sunglasses—of course, the sunglasses—in place.

Ada had told me to clean the house out. I had accepted the order but that didn't mean I had to like it. I had no qualms about killing because killing was business. Falzarano was a target. Like Ellis had been. The job was the job and that's what we got paid to do.

But this was something different. Cleaning the house meant taking out the targets and then everyone else. And there was a whole lot of everyone and now I knew they weren't quite what they looked like. As I stood and considered my options at the top of the stairs more guards appeared and ran around the driveway and the fountain and off up to the main gate out of sight and off around the side of the house and off into the trees around us. Dogs barked and footsteps crunched.

Falzarano—or at least something that looked a good deal *like* Falzarano—was asleep in the hidden computer room. He was an easy mark, the job I was supposed to do. I figured he could sit just where he was until I was ready for him.

In the meantime I wanted to find out just what was going on. I didn't like the job Ada had given to me. I didn't like the way it coincided with the arrival of the intruders, none of whom I'd actually seen yet.

Ada knew something I didn't. And I had a feeling the new arrivals did too.

I made it down to the fountain and went to pick a direction to sniff in when Alfie jogged around from the other side. When he saw me he jerked his head to one side.

"Come on," he said. "We'll take the back." He pulled the gun that had once belonged to Stefano from the back of his pants and he led the way.

I followed. Alfie's plan was a good one. With all the focus at the front of the house it seemed like a good idea to go help out with the others securing the rear of the property.

Not that that was what I was planning on doing. Getting Alfie around the back of the house meant I'd have the chance to ask him a few questions.

And the woods looked like a good place to hide a body.

Alfie walked ahead of me, gun hanging loosely in one hand, cigarette magically stuck to his bottom lip. We moved past the garage and ducked down a path between the palm trees and then we were on the big lawn by the side of the house. I looked up at the castle and looked at the trellis that led up to the window of the room that Emerson Ellis had been put in.

How Ellis had ended up in the piano I didn't know but clearly he *had* come down the side of the building. The damage to the trellis and the vegetation was too good to be staged. So he'd escaped, made a break for it, perhaps timing his run with the guard patrols he'd watched from his window like I had. Then he was away, most likely across the lawn, over the small wall, into the thick stand of pines that Alfie and I were now heading toward. The pines were a good place to hide.

Except he'd met someone in the pines. The evidence said it was a guard, one Ellis had clobbered with a rock. If he'd done that—if he'd been capable of it—then his route might have been clear. It was a difficult way back through the trees to civilization but a desperate man was capable of many difficult things.

Did that include killing a guard? I doubted it. And I doubted it even more considering Emerson Ellis had not escaped through the pines. He'd been killed and his body had been taken back inside and hidden in the piano.

So Ellis hadn't killed a guard. Someone else had. The same someone who killed Ellis and stashed his body. The piano was a good place to hide it. Even if Ellis had met his fate in the pine trees, come morning his body or his freshly dug grave would have been found by the dogs. The piano was an especially good place to hide him if his death had been ordered by Carmina. She would have needed help to get him in. Help from the person who had killed him.

From the person I was now following into the pine trees.

Alfie Micklewhite. Francis Cane. The man from International Automatic.

There was nobody else it could have been. And if Alfie was responsible for the death of Emerson Ellis, there was more than a fair chance he was responsible for the death of Vaughan Delaney as well.

Which meant Carmina and Alfie weren't helping Falzarano build a factory. They were trying to *stop* him.

And *why* they wanted to stop him was the question I was planning on putting to Alfie in person.

Except by the time I turned around from observing the side of the house, Alfie had left me on the lawn and had disappeared into the pine trees already.

I followed.

The farther I got from the house the quieter it got, the sounds of the guards running and shouting and the dogs barking getting fainter and fainter and melting into the sounds of crickets and owls and twigs crunching underfoot. If there were trespassers somewhere in the trees around me they were doing a better job of staying quiet than I was.

The dull glow of the pale moonlit night plunged into an inky blackness once I was among the pines. It was a great place to hide in and it seemed like a weakness of Falzarano's secluded property. He had a lot of guns and a long driveway, but if you could get in from the side you could almost get right up to the house under a good deal of cover.

I turned my optics up and kept going. The ground sloped

downward and the slope was getting steeper. I'd been out ten minutes. There was no sign of Alfie and I hadn't found his trail either. I stopped and listened but there was nothing much to listen to and I certainly hadn't heard any shooting yet. I'd come the wrong way, clearly. The intruders weren't on this side of the house at all.

I turned and started back up the slope and then I heard a crack. I turned toward the noise, cycling my optics through a series of filters to try to get some kind of clear signal, but it was too dark and my optical light was too bright and all I got was a snowy sort of fuzz in pinks and greens.

But somewhere in that storm I saw something move, a shape that was nothing more than a silhouette but one shaped rather like a man. Whoever he was he was hunched over, trying to keep a low profile. His outline was long, like he was wearing a coat, and he had a hat on and he was carrying something in an outstretched arm.

A gun. A big one too, although it was hard to be sure given that I couldn't see anything properly yet.

But whoever it was it wasn't Alfie because Alfie wasn't wearing a hat or a coat.

One of the intruders. On his own, a scout sent around from the main party, just to watch the house. It was hard to see, but maybe the hat and maybe the coat matched the ones worn by the men in the car we'd sent rocketing down the valley. This guy was heading up to the house through the pines and he was moving quietly, his footfalls cushioned by the thick bed of brown needles. He was a good deal more fleet-footed than I was, although he was also half my size and a tenth the weight.

I slipped behind a tree then peeked out the other side to

get a better look. I blinked and my optics began to clear faster, but when they were clear the intruder was nowhere in sight.

I turned to head back up the hill at a diagonal. If Alfie was still somewhere on this side of the house then with a bit of luck the intruder would be between us.

There was a snap behind me, followed by a crash. I spun around and saw someone else approaching. He was also in a hat but the overcoat was missing and the gun he was carrying was long and thin. A rifle. One of Falzarano's boys, having made his way around from the front of the house. He hadn't seen me and he was headed on down the hill through the pines.

I turned and tried to gauge the direction of my target but there was no movement ahead and only the sound of the guard crashing around somewhere behind me.

I headed up the hill, slipping in the loamy dirt. In a few minutes I was higher up the hill but the pine trees were just as thick and I couldn't find any trail so I kept going and trusted I was headed in the right direction. After ten minutes the glow of the houselights began to light my horizon and I could see the hard edge of the low wall that ran alongside the big lawn. I moved to one side and a branch came into the line of my optics and blocked out the light.

That's when I saw him.

He was lying against that same wall, his back to me, his head tucked in and his arms pressed together. He was wearing a black suit and a black hat and in the right angle formed by the wall and the ground he was dressed pretty well for camouflage so long as it remained dark.

I crouched down beside him and grabbed his shoulder.

He rolled over without any resistance and his arms flopped around. His eyes were open, which was not a good sign but I checked anyway and sure enough he was dead.

I didn't know who he was. His suit was black, likewise his hat and his tie. His shirt was white but when I opened his jacket to check for identification I saw the shirt was staining another color on the man's left side, down around the kidney. I checked it. The shirt had a tear in it and there was a corresponding slot cut in the man's side.

He'd been killed. Like Coke Patterson had been killed.

I thought he'd been carrying a gun when I saw him before but he wasn't carrying it now and a quick look around told me he hadn't dropped it. He hadn't just been stabbed and fallen against the wall either. The tracks in the pine needles were clear. He'd been dragged and dumped by the wall in a rough attempt to hide him.

Inside his jacket pocket was a roll of breath mints and a clean handkerchief and a wallet. The wallet had nothing but a two-dollar bill in it and a charge card for a department store downtown.

I checked the pocket opposite and found something else. Another wallet, a bifold a good deal smaller than the other one. I flipped it open and a rectangular piece of stiff card about the size of a matchbox cover fell out. While I reached down to pick it up I looked at the wallet. On each side was a clear plastic insert and behind one was a piece of printed card and behind the other was a photograph.

The man in the photograph was the same man now lying at my feet. According to the card in the other fold of the wallet, his name was Jackson Waid and he was a special agent with the Department of Robot Labor. The identification card was signed at the bottom by both Jackson Waid and his boss, Special Agent Touch Daley.

I stared at the card for quite a while. My optics followed the curl of Touch Daley's signature and for a moment I saw a man standing on a rooftop and then he and the rooftop were gone.

The other piece of card that had fallen out of the wallet was cut to the right size to be slipped behind the plastic of an ID wallet just like the one belonging to Jackson Waid. I was looking at the back of it so I turned it around.

It was a photograph. Same as Jackson Waid's. Same hat. Same suit. Same firm expressionless expression. The photograph of another special agent from the Department of Robot Labor. There was no identification card with the photograph, but I bet it would have been signed by Special Agent Touch Daley as well.

Only I didn't need the card to know who the agent was. I'd seen him before. Once in Falzarano's house and then again as he lay cooling in his own bed.

The man was Coke Patterson.

I pocketed the photograph and then I headed back toward the house. I'd wasted enough time now.

I had a job to do.

36

The house was quiet and empty. All the guards were now outside. I still hadn't heard any gunfire and as I'd crunched across the gravel of the driveway things seemed to have calmed down. Falzarano's boys weren't running quite as fast as they had been. I wasn't sure that was actually a good thing. If things were settling in for a siege then that was going to make things difficult for me. Difficult was not something I liked.

And now I knew why Ada wanted me to get out fast. Because the new arrivals were agents from the Department of Robot Labor. Back in the day, DORL had been a part of the federal government, overseeing the robot program of the 1950s that had changed the world and ultimately led to the creation of myself and Ada, work for which the department's chief roboticist, Professor C. Thornton, PhD, had been personally responsible.

And the world had got unchanged and DORL was mothballed along with all its products. All, that is, except me. I was the last robot built and my program was allowed to run. I was a private detective doing a good job and Ada was doing an even better one.

Especially once she figured out that killing people paid more than helping them.

And now someone had brought DORL out of cold storage, and I had a feeling I knew that already because the name Touch Daley rang a particular kind of bell somewhere. He and his reactivated department had gotten wind of something going on at Falzarano's hillside hideout. So they sent in an agent, Coke Patterson, to find out what. And find out he did, only for someone to find *him* out. Whether that was before or after he'd gotten word back to his own boss, I didn't know, but DORL clearly missed him and had issued standard departmental ID photos to their other agents so they'd know who they were looking for. If DORL thought he was missing then they couldn't have found his body. Someone must have cleaned up Patterson's apartment. I hadn't seen a piano in there so his body must have been hidden somewhere else.

The question was, who had discovered Coke Patterson's secret? Falzarano might have had a suspicion. He'd sent me and Alfie over to Patterson's apartment to give him a fright, only someone had got there first. Maybe the same someone who'd gotten to Vaughan Delaney. Maybe Emerson Ellis too. My prime suspect was Alfie, but he'd looked as surprised as I'd felt back at Patterson's place.

Alfie, the man who was working under an assumed name, who said he had come to Hollywood, California to become a movie star.

I had a sudden feeling he was a better actor than he said he was.

None of this mattered much to me at this particular juncture and I knew that come the morning I wouldn't remember a thing about it anyway. I had a job to do and that job had been made difficult by the arrival of DORL.

I had to get in and get out, quick. To hell with the rest. Cleaning the house would have been difficult before, but it was impossible now, so Ada would have to make do with the original job and she'd like it.

Inside Falzarano's house I crossed the checkerboard entrance hall and headed toward Falzarano's study. There was nobody there. The books were scattered behind the desk where I had left them and the hidden door was closed as I had left it.

I walked over and jammed a finger on the button on the bookcase. The bookcase clicked and swung open an inch like it had before and I swung it open some more and headed down the secret passage behind it to the computer room.

The doors were closed so I opened them and stepped inside. It was all still there, with one exception.

Falzarano.

His alcove was empty and the fat gray cable was hooked onto the console next to it. The alcove next to his was empty as it had been before. Stefano reposed in the third.

"What are you doing here?" A woman's voice, heavy with a foreign accent and something else too, the words coming fast, loud. It was the voice of a woman who was not afraid, but who knew the current situation was not as she wanted it and was about to get worse.

Carmina was standing not in the main doorway but in

another one on my left, the white panel sliding shut behind her like it wasn't a door at all. She was still wearing the white lab coat over her dress and she looked surprised to see me. She walked slowly toward me, looking up and down all the while like she hadn't seen me before in her life. The way she moved told me she had no idea of who was banging on the gates.

"The thing I can't figure out," I said, "is whether the men from the Department of Robot Labor are here for you or the old man. I'm thinking both." I waved around the computer room. "And they sure as hell are going to love all this. Quite the operation. You brought the plans with you from Colombia and you used Falzarano's deep pockets to recreate it all in California? Isn't that right, Professor Blanco?"

Carmina stopped and raised an eyebrow and then a smile appeared. It wasn't the trademark curl of before because this time it was the real thing.

"You are remarkably well informed," she said.

"I have a remarkably good source," I said. "Falzarano. Where is he?"

"Why do you want to know?" She took a step away from me but she was slow and I was fast. I grabbed her wrist. She yelped in surprise. Then she pulled but my grip was firm. I squeezed her wrist. She yelped again and this time it was in pain.

"You're hurting me."

"The old man. Now."

She scowled and pulled with her arm but I didn't let go. The scowl turned into a hiss and she nodded back to the wall panel she'd stepped through before.

"He's in there."

I moved over and I pulled the professor with me.

"But he's not ready to be moved," she said. I stopped where I was and I looked down at her. "Not yet, anyway."

Moving him wasn't on my itemized agenda so I ignored her and continued to the door. Carmina complained all the way.

I went through the doorway and into a short white corridor. The wall at the end slid open as I approached. I went through and I pulled Carmina with me.

The room beyond was like the computer room except it was missing the computers. It was square with a blue ceiling and white walls and a white floor. Instead of mainframes lining the walls, the room was lined with shelves. There were more shelves running in four rows down the center of the room. There was a single computer console against one room covered in flashing lights. It had a telephone handset built into it.

It was a storage room, not entirely unlike the storage room back at my office.

Except what was being stored in this room was not memory tapes, boxed and labeled and saved for a rainy day.

The room was storing something else entirely.

I let go of Carmina and I walked up to the shelf nearest. I cast my eye up and down and I slowly walked along the shelves.

They were heads. They were all metal. Some were big and some were small. Some were square, nothing more than upturned buckets. Some were more elegantly sculpted. Some had lenses and grilles. Some had a vague approximation of human features. Triangular noses and triangular eyebrows and cheekbones machined from steel and titanium and other metals in other colors.

I kept walking. I forgot all about Carmina. All I could think about were the heads.

Robot heads. There were dozens of them. Maybe even hundreds. All lined up on the shelves, shelves that filled the whole room.

I stepped closer to the head nearest. It had a dark bronzed finish, like my own skin. The top of the head was flat. The eyes were two round saucers that looked ceramic. The mouth was a row of ceramic squares, eight of them lined up underneath a nose that looked like the folded wings of a paper airplane.

The shelf had a label on it, just below the head. It said DORL-88-55.

I looked at the heads next to it. On this shelf they were all almost the same, just a slight variance in condition more than anything. Some looked new—DORL-88-55 included. Some looked a little rough, a little bent at the edges, a little rusty around the ceramic eye dishes.

They were all labeled DORL.

I stepped back. I looked around. Every head had a label. The whole collection was catalogued.

"Ah, my friend Ray, my good friend Ray, how pleased I am that you are here, ah, ah, ah?"

I turned at the voice, a voice I recognized, a voice that belonged to an old man I had once saved from certain death and whom I'd last seen plugged into a computer bank like me.

Like a robot.

Falzarano walked toward me, glancing at the shelves around him, trailing a finger along the labels. He looked good, back to his old self, which I put down to the fact that he was still plugged in at the chest. Except it wasn't to a computer bank, it was to a metal briefcase that hung in his right hand, the cable from his chest connecting to a port on the flat side. He must have seen me looking at the case because he lifted it up and tapped it with the underside of a ring on his other hand.

"Thank you for the vital components," he said. "Thank you, thank you, thank you. You arrived just in time, my friend, my good friend. Just in time."

Right then I felt the mark on my back plate like it was as wide and as deep as the Grand Canyon and my diagnostic log pushed a message loud and clear into my central processor.

Error 66.

"Don't tell me," I said, and then I nodded at Carmina. "Your friendly scientist needed parts, and quick, but she couldn't get me open in time. Hence a quick, if unexpected, shopping trip to Thornton's lab."

For a moment I thought I remembered two voices, a man and a woman, the pair not quite arguing but their conversation getting a little on the hot side as they fussed around by my back plate.

Then it was gone, a fragment overwritten in a microsecond. Error 66 sure had done a number on my memory tape.

Carmina just smiled and lifted her chin in a way that was both noncommittal and entirely guilty. She didn't seem to feel like talking so I kept going.

"Of course I don't know how it's done," I said. "I had a look at our old friend Stefano. He seems dead enough.

Then there was the other guard killed during Ellis's escape. So they're still people. Improved perhaps, a little electronic wizardry here and there, but still people. Mr. Falzarano, on the other hand—well, if this is some kind of electronic immortality you've come up with then I have to congratulate you, Professor Blanco. I'm sure the folk outside are going to want a very long conversation about your work."

At this Falzarano laughed and the smile fixed on Carmina's face flickered and when it came back on it was perhaps a little dimmer than before.

I gestured to the shelf behind me. "Quite a collection you have here," I said.

Falzarano nodded. "I wish I could have shown you all of this with, shall we say, a little more . . . preparation. But no matter, Ray, no matter." Falzarano looked around. His face broke into a grin. "But I am glad you appreciate it all. This is the place I keep my special treasures. There are examples here of nearly every machine that your federal robot program produced before that program was ended. March twenty-sixth, 1959. And after that, all the robots were recalled and destroyed."

He paused and laid a hand on the face of one of the heads, a silver thing that was nearly spherical with no optics or other features. "But, such things, they take time, Ray, my friend, they take time. Many machines had been made. The recall was a huge operation, huge. So I was able to save these myself—these are all the central processing units, you understand, yes?" He tapped the silver head. "Within, Thornton's miracle machine, the positronic computational brain. It has taken me many years of searching and much of my fortune to salvage these parts, but my collection is nearly complete."

"Nearly complete?"

"Why, yes, Ray, my son."

Falzarano moved across the shelf to the one I was at. He pointed to a space at the end of the row. Room enough for another head. There was already a label in place below where the new artifact would sit.

"DORL-26-59a," he read. Then he turned to me. Behind him, Carmina pushed herself off the wall and unfolded her arms. Her curled smile was brighter than ever.

"Also known," Falzarano continued, "as Raymond Electromatic."

37

I read the label on the shelf.

DORL-26-59a

Department of Robot Labor Enterprise Project 26-59a.

Or in other words, the last robot ever built. Raymond Electromatic, onetime private detective, full-time private assassin.

Falzarano clapped his hands again. I turned from the shelf to him and he nodded and smiled like I thought his plan to add me to his collection was as sweet as apple pie.

"But what do you want all this for?" I asked. I pointed at his steel briefcase. "If you're a robot, or at least partially one, then you're nothing like what Thornton built for the program. Everything in your collection is hardened alloys and electric circuits. Just like me, DORL-26-59a. But you—you are anything but. Whatever is keeping you going is years, decades ahead of the DORL."

Falzarano nodded and pursed his lips. Carmina leaned against the old man's side and did some more of that head tilting like she couldn't help it. Falzarano smiled at her and patted her head.

"You were right, at least partially," she said. "What did you call it? Electronic immortality? You are close, but even you would not be able to understand the techniques I have developed."

Falzarano nodded and looked up at me. "Do you know how old I am, Ray, ah, ah? Well, let me tell you. Next week I turn one hundred and one years."

He held a finger up in the air like he was silencing an objection I just hadn't had time to think of yet.

"Oh yes, oh yes," he said. "People, they live to this age. This is not magic. But I have old bones, my friend, old bones. I should be dead a long time now. A long time now."

"Except you aren't," I said.

Carmina smiled and gave Falzarano a little kiss on the cheek. "Electronic immortality," she said, "so long as we can get the right parts."

I frowned on the inside. "So that's why you need her," I said. "An expert roboticist, one perhaps with political, maybe criminal, leanings in your direction. She supposedly dies in the Colombian Civil War so you can bring her back here to keep you alive and well in the heart of Hollywood."

Carmina laughed. "Very astute."

"Astute is hardwired into my permanent store."

Carmina laughed again.

"But while she's here," I continued, "you get her to work on something else. Maybe it was the original plan before you got sidetracked with saving your own life. It started with this collection. How long did it take to get all the heads? Years?" I turned to the shelf nearest and looked at the faces of my brothers. "You salvaged the heads because that's what you needed. Get enough of them, maybe you could extract Thornton's master programs. My creator was one of a kind, a genius. Nobody could match him. So you use your organization to make Professor Carmen Blanco an offer. Come to America, help design and build a robot factory. She's got the know-how, you've got the money. A man with your means, it's easy. You pay off Vaughan Delaney at the city planning office to get permission to build the factory somewhere where nobody will bat an eyelid, and you hire Emerson Ellis's company to build it. I guess you probably used both of them for work before. You have your claws hooked pretty deep all over Los Angeles, after all."

Falzarano nodded and then he opened his arms and looked around the shelves.

"One hundred and twelve positronic computational units. One hundred and twelve pieces of Thornton's master program." He pulled himself off Carmina and went back to the big silver robot head. He laid a hand on its curved dome, fingers splayed like he was feeling for phrenological bumps, and he narrowed his eyes. "Inside each and every one of these electric brains are the secrets, yes? Each and every one contains the blueprints and the master program for themselves. That is why the electric brain is so important." He curled his hand into a fist and knocked on the top of the silver head. "If I can get in here and break the codes, yes, yes, then those secrets will be mine. And with my factory I will be able to make my own robots, ah?

Think of that, my son, think of that. Those men out there, my men—yes, they are men. True, they are, how shall we say . . . *altered*. But they are still men. Unreliable, expensive men. What I have to pay them! Ah! What better than to have men made out of metal. Men I can control, who do not need to be paid, who do not need to sleep or eat or drink. Who are not distracted, ah? Who are incapable of betrayal, ah?"

I nodded. "Oh, I get it, believe me. The perfect gang. The robot mafia. But you haven't quite cracked it yet, have you? Thornton encrypted his code well enough." I walked along the shelf. I looked at the robot heads. All DORL salvage. All supposedly destroyed when the federal government cancelled the robot program. Falzarano's collection seemed pretty big, but the federal robot program had produced tens of thousands of machines of all different sorts over the course of a decade. Despite his proud boast, Falzarano's little stash only represented a tiny fraction of the total.

But even so.

"Thing is," I said, "possession of robot parts is a federal crime." I turned back to the professor and her mentor. "And the Department of Robot Labor isn't as decommissioned as you might think." I pointed to the door. "They're here, now, and I have a feeling they want all this back. I don't know if they knew it was all here, not unless their mole found your secret door. He was here about your factory plans. All this? This might be a bonus. Who knows. I guess we'll find out soon enough." I stepped closer to Carmina. "It was probably a bad idea, sending me and Alfie to Thornton's old lab. They must have had the place under surveillance, after the accident that got it all sealed up. They'd been watching this house for a while and then they find me and Alfie breaking into the lab. They knew something was happening, maybe faster than they thought, especially after their agent on the inside suddenly becomes incommunicado. I hate to say it, but I think the game is up, folks."

"How right you are, Charlie."

I turned my head at the voice and Falzarano and Carmina turned theirs too.

Alfie Micklewhite came walking into the storage room, smile on his face and big gun in his hand. Only it wasn't the gun he'd taken from Stefano but something entirely different, something made of silver and glass, with an odd fat barrel shaped like a pinecone, the size and shape about right for the gun I'd seen the DORL agent carrying out in the woods before Alfie had killed him and stolen the weapon. Inside the glass pinecone were densely packed filaments and wires. I didn't know what the gun did exactly but it was pointed in my direction and I had no immediate plans to find out what would happen to me if he squeezed the trigger.

Alfie moved over to Carmina and Falzarano. The professor and her mentor didn't seem too agitated. I still didn't know why Francis Cane was calling himself Alfie Micklewhite or what International Automatic was, but it was clear that he was in on it with the other two.

That was when the telephone began to ring.

It was on the console behind me. It rang twice more and nobody moved. Then it rang a third time and Alfie flicked his wrist and the gun held in that hand.

"Answer it, Charlie, will you?" he said.

"What if it isn't for me?"

Alfie laughed. He adjusted his glasses with his free hand. "Of course it's bloody well for you, isn't it? Your boss, the lovely Ada. Answer it then pass me over."

I watched the big gun in Alfie's hand as I picked up the telephone. There was one question on my mind and I think Ada knew just what it was.

"Well, you have to admit, it was worth a shot," she said.

"Ada," I said.

"I guess it was insurance, more than anything. A preemptive strike, isn't that what they call it?"

"Who is it?"

"I think I read about that in *Time* magazine one time."

"Ada, who is it?"

"Or was it *Harper's*?"

Alfie's eyes narrowed. He cocked his head, like he was trying to hear what Ada was saying. Which was impossible for him, of course. He waved his free hand at me to get me to hand the telephone over. That wasn't going to work either so I just ignored him.

"Who's the client, Ada?"

"Ray—"

"Who's the client. Tell me."

Ada sighed. "Okay, fine, you want in, you get in."

She took a healthy draw on her cigarette. She held it a long time and then she breathed it out.

"It's me, Ray," she said.

Somewhere I heard the ticking of the fast hand of a stopwatch.

"The client is me."

38

"Oi, that's enough of that, Charlie."

Alfie snatched the telephone out of my hand. He waved his magic gun at me and I backed away while he put the phone to his ear.

"Hello? Ada? You listening?"

Alfie frowned and I saw his eyes narrow behind his glasses. I could imagine what he was hearing on the phone: nothing but the roar of the sea, far away. That was part of Thornton's trick, part of the design of a robot and his computer who had to talk to each other over the public telephone system. Fill the line with noise and you can hide another signal in there, one that only Ada and I can hear. Proof against bugs and wiretappers and people with magic guns and bad tempers.

Alfie laughed. He looked up at me. He drew the mouthpiece of the telephone up to his lips.

"I assume you can hear me even if I can't hear you. Listen, love, I've been dying to have a little chat, I really have. You're a clever girl, I can see that. But here's the thing. You tapped IA to get information on me. Which is just fine and dandy, but I'm not sure you did your sums right. Because that meant IA could tap you. See, that means we know where you are, and I've got your fella right here in front of me. Sending him in here to do your dirty work . . . well, I'm not one to judge, am I? He's the one with the legs, after all. I must admit it was a surprise him turning up like that, but I think IA are going to be pretty happy with him. And you of course, darling. Might be in line for a promotion after all this, eh?"

Alfie laughed, then he tore his head away from the telephone as a deafening whine of feedback echoed down the line.

"Yeah, love you too," he said, holding the hand piece at arm's length. Then he brought the speaking end back to his mouth. "I'll be seeing you." He made a kissing noise into the phone then he yanked the handset away from the console. The spiral cable stretched, then snapped like a piece of elastic. He threw the handset into the opposite corner of the storeroom.

I looked at the gun and I looked at Falzarano and Carmina. The pair was standing by Alfie. She looked pretty happy about the situation. Falzarano, less so. He looked at Alfie.

"What's this, ah, ah? IA? But IA is—"

"International Automatic," I said. I nodded at Alfie. "Your boy here is a company man, name of Francis Cane."

Falzarano turned his head from me to Alfie—to *Francis*—and back again several times, jaw slack, jowls a-quiver.

IA. International Automatic. A robotics company. One

with an apparent interest in me and Ada. But how he fitted into Falzarano's organization I didn't know.

I looked at Alfie's gun again. Whatever it shot it wasn't likely to be bullets. I had a feeling it was exactly the kind of gun you'd use against a robot. It probably beamed some kind of electromagnetic pulse, something that would tangle my circuits and scramble my processors and knock me out cold, if not worse.

I remembered something about the Hollywood sign and for a moment I saw a girl with black hair and thick black rings of makeup around her eyes like an Egyptian princess.

And then she was gone and I was looking at Alfie Micklewhite.

"What do you mean, you know where Ada is?" I asked. "The Electromatic Detective Agency is in the telephone directory. Look it up, I'll give you the tour."

Alfie cocked his head. "Oh, you mean that thing back at your office? All them bells and whistles? You think that's Ada, eh? Ah well, not as clever a detective as you thought you were, eh?"

I didn't say anything. As a matter of fact, I did think that Ada was back at the office. That was where Professor Thornton had put us, after all. Just a robot and his computer going about their business.

I thought about this for fifty-two microseconds. I thought about the sounds of Ada smoking, of her drinking coffee. I thought about her laugh.

They were nothing. Echoes. Fragments. A ghost in the machine, images, sensations, inadvertently imprinted on my template, the template that Professor Thornton had based on his own mind.

And then I thought about an older woman with big hair, smoking in the office, telling a younger couple how to reconnect something electrical as I lay in my alcove unable to move.

Was that an echo too?

Or was that something else.

A . . . memory?

"But, Alfie, my boy, my boy, I do not understand." Falzarano had moved around, until he was almost standing on my side of the foursome. Perhaps unconsciously Carmina moved closer to Alfie at the same time. "What does International Automatic want here?"

"I would have thought that was as clear as crystal," I said. "IA wants your factory, the plans, the works." I looked at Carmina. "They want your roboticist too."

Carmina cocked her head at me. "I have been in partnership with Mr. Cane and International Automatic for years. IA have been trying to break into the secrets of the old federal robot program in your country for just as long. With Falzarano's collection in their possession, they will finally be able to decode Thornton's master program."

"A collection which now includes you, Charlie," said Alfie. "Oh, and Ada, too. That'll make it much easier. Of course it would have been much easier to just keep Mr. Falzarano's operation going like we planned, but now we'll just have to take the factory plans, and IA will have to try and get it built somewhere else. Still, it could be worse, eh?"

Falzarano looked at me and I looked at him and then I looked at Alfie.

"Handy," I said, "having DORL knock at the door. Covers you pretty well."

Alfie sniffed and checked his watch. Then he looked back at me.

"Covers me for what?"

"Your own incompetence," I said. "Because if you wanted Falzarano's factory operation, then killing Vaughan Delaney and Emerson Ellis is a strange way of going about it. Taking those two out would have played havoc with the schedule."

Alfie grinned. "I don't know if you remember, but Vaughan Delaney jumped out of a tall building. If you're saying I had anything to do with that you need your circuits rewired."

If I could have raised an eyebrow I would have. "I'm sure. Of course you had an accomplice. The piano was a good place to hide Emerson Ellis, at least until you could figure out a way of disposing of the body, so long as nobody played it. Carmina is the only pianist among us, so that took care of that."

Something flickered between Alfie and Carmina. She shook her head a little and then Alfie raised his gun a fraction higher.

"What are you on about? Ellis is missing. You saying someone stashed him in the bleeding piano—"

Gunfire erupted, close by. It was followed by shouting and the sound of running feet. Then more gunshots and more shouts and then it was very quiet.

We were out of time and I knew it. I said the same to Alfie and he gave me a scowl while Carmina went to the door of the storeroom and peered beyond it.

"DORL aren't going to let you out of here," I said. "They're here to reclaim their property, and that includes me."

Alfie shook his head. "Not likely, Charlie. See, I've got something they haven't, which is you. And you're exactly what I need."

"What, you hope to negotiate your way out of this mess?"

"No, no, come on, Charlie, use that calculator you have for a brain. I know what you did for the old man, at that place downtown. You can protect us. Now, let me see . . ."

He glanced around the storeroom. Then his gaze settled on the big silver spherical robot head. "Yeah, that'll do," he said, pointing with his gun. "We'll take that one. As the old man said, each and every one of these things holds the entire master program of the federal robot project. All I need is one of them."

I chuckled. It sounded like a truck starting on a cold winter's morning and it made Alfie flick the gun again.

"Something funny, Charlie?"

"Oh, lots of things," I said. "But you're overlooking something."

"Oh yeah, what's that, eh?"

"I might be bulletproof," I said, "but DORL also have plenty of guns that don't shoot bullets. Like that piece you got off the agent in the woods. I have a feeling they were made just for an occasion like this one."

Alfie stepped up to me and the gun never wavered. "All the better, then, ain't it? They won't want to damage the last robot in the world, now will they?" The gun twitched in his grip. "Time to move. You pick up that head, then lead the way out. The old man after you. He's got enough gizmos inside him for this thing to work just as well as it would on you, Charlie."

I looked at Falzarano. He was shaking his head, muttering something under his breath in his native tongue.

I went to the shelf and picked up the big round silver head. I wondered who it belonged to. I wondered if in another world we might have been friends.

I looked at Alfie and he waved the gun. I nodded and headed toward the door. Falzarano followed. Alfie next with Carmina behind him.

As we got closer to the gunfire I wondered what it was exactly that people had against robots.

What were they afraid of?

And what was Ada afraid of? Because she didn't want Falzarano to build his factory and she didn't want IA to get the master program either. She'd concocted this whole elaborate plan, in the guise of another job. Insurance, she called it. Against what? This wasn't about people finding out about our new line of work.

This was much, much bigger than that, and I wasn't even considering what Alfie had said about knowing where Ada was.

Where she *really* was.

The main computer room was humming with power as we walked in. Every system was active. A test program, perhaps, being run by Carmina, in a copy of her lab back in Colombia that would eventually be needed to run Falzarano's factory.

The factory that would have needed its own power station. The thing about computers and robots is that they needed a lot of juice. The computer room was alive with a lot of high voltage. A lot of high voltage indeed.

I stopped in the middle of the room, the big silver head

in my arms. I looked down at it. It was dead, and it had no face. All I could see was the distorted reflection of my own in the curved surface.

"Oi! Move it, Charlie!"

I turned around. Falzarano was behind me and watching without a sound, and behind him, Alfie and Carmina stepped through the door to the storage room. Alfie held the gun on me as he half-turned to fiddle with the sliding door control with his other hand. Out of habit, most likely.

It was a mistake, of course.

I tossed the silver head at Alfie. He ducked down and fired his magic gun, but he was well off target. Falzarano was in front of me and he caught the blast.

The old man's back exploded in a shower of sparks. He groaned and fell against one of the computer consoles. Then his half-human body sparked again, enough to set the console shorting underneath him. The console fizzed and then exploded and the hum of power in the room went up more than a few decibels.

Alfie yelled something and lifted his gun again to fire a second time. I ducked to one side and he squeezed the trigger. He missed me but the blast caught one of the computer banks. The front of it exploded and flames began to lick out of the exposed circuitry behind.

"*Idiota!*" Carmina yelled, arms raised in front of her face as the computer consoles sparked like the Fourth of July. "His head! All we need is his head, take it!"

There was a bang. And then another. Carmina twisted in the air, the front of her lab coat popping with red as she was torn up by gunshots.

Falzarano slumped back onto the floor, 1938 Mauser

Schnellfeuer sliding out of his hand. Alfie's gun, the one that had jammed, the one he had left with Stefano's body.

A body transferred to the computer room for Carmina's robot experiment.

Another console exploded. Alfie stood by the storeroom door, his magic gun loose in his hand. One of the lenses of his glasses was chipped and his wavy hair was curling up along the edge.

I ran toward him. I looked into his eyes. I grabbed the wrist behind the gun. He offered no resistance.

More gunfire from outside. The DORL agents would be at the main office any time.

The fire was hot and getting hotter. It would consume the whole house, including Falzarano's collection, including Falzarano himself and the body of Professor Carmen Blanco.

I looked around the burning computer room. The machinery in the room was big. Computers the size of refrigerators, the size of the kind of truck you'd deliver a refrigerator *in*. There was no way it had all been brought in through the house.

Alfie coughed, and didn't stop coughing. I didn't need to breathe but the smoke wasn't any good for him.

And I wanted him alive just a little bit longer.

"There a way out the back?" I asked.

Alfie nodded as he heaved for breath, his hand fumbling for the sliding door controls. I knocked his hand away and got the door open. Then Alfie stumbled onward into the clear air of the storeroom.

I followed.

39

I drove through the hills and Alfie sat next to me. We drove in a thick, syrupy silence punctuated only by sporadic fits of coughing from my passenger that were just as heavy. It was nearly dawn. The sky was stars above and an orange band of light at the horizon and my time was nearly up.

The fire from the computer lab spread quickly and was licking at our heels as we came up out of a sunken loading bay at the back of Falzarano's castle. The fire was a good distraction for Falzarano's remaining men and the agents from DORL alike. Alfie and I made it through the pines, then I followed his head as we looped back around and came into the garage through a side door concealed from the driveway.

Once we were in the Buick we were fine, because the Buick was a special car. Reinforced, if not entirely armored. It made short work of the garage door and neither

Falzarano's boys nor the men from the DORL were fast enough to stop us as we powered up the driveway. Up on the main road were several black cars but none of them were ready to roll when we blasted past them and it was easy enough to shake the two that finally managed to get off their starting blocks. By the time that had happened we were too far ahead and the hill roads were steep and winding and there was a lot of them and I used every turn to my advantage, making sure the tails stayed shaken.

I was good at my job. I was programmed to be.

Falzarano was dead. Carmina was dead. Whatever was left after the fire, the DORL were welcome to it. Better for it to be in their hands than in the hands of IA.

That just left Alfie Micklewhite, real name, Francis Cane. The IA agent, if not entirely well then at least still breathing in the seat next to me.

A man with more than a few questions to answer. But not about himself or IA or the factory or anything else.

No, I was interested in something else entirely.

Ada.

Alfie had said that IA had found her. When I expressed a certain level of surprise, Alfie had said that Ada wasn't at my office. He'd said that the computer room was . . . well, whatever it was, it wasn't what I thought it was.

It wasn't Ada. Ada, he'd said, was somewhere else. And IA knew where.

I wanted to know too.

We came around a corner. The hills were still high but there were fewer of them now as we approached the edge of the city. I pulled the car around the next bend. Our destination was just ahead, a dirt access road that I knew I had been on before, one that led to a makeshift parking lot cut into the hillside beside a green hut and behind a giant sign with letters forty feet high that looked out across the whole damn city.

I pulled in beside the hut. Alfie coughed and squinted ahead and then he sat up with a start, which set off another coughing fit. This didn't stop him reaching inside his jacket for a packet of cigarettes.

"Where the bloody hell are we, eh?"

I killed the car. The telephone rang next to me. I knew who it was. I picked up.

"Ray?"

"Loose ends, Ada, loose ends."

I hung up. I put the phone down. I turned to Alfie sitting next to me.

"You and I are going to have a certain kind of conversation, Alfie."

He looked at me from behind his thick glasses. He blinked, he placed a cigarette between his lips and smiled.

"You got a light, Charlie?"

I lifted my fingers and ignited a spark and when, a little while later, I drove back down into Hollywood I was driving alone.

40

"You're very quiet."

I looked up into the corner of the computer room. All around me Ada's lights flashed and her computers hummed and the reels of tape spun ever onwards.

I didn't say anything because I didn't know what to say. So I got back to work. Ada blew smoke around my circuits and when I was done I folded the sheet of yellow legal paper in half lengthwise and slipped it in between the pages of the paperback book that was sitting on the small table. Then I took that book and I put it into the inside pocket of my short black trench coat that was over the back of the chair I was sitting on.

"Lottery numbers, Ray?" Ada asked. "Or do you have a good tip on a fast horse?"

I stood up. I looked at the clock over the door. It was either late or very early, depending on your point of view.

"Listen, chief, if it's about the job, then you'll understand why I had to do it."

I got into my alcove.

"Insurance, Ray. A bit of initiative, that's all. The bull and the horns and all that jazz."

I looked at the window opposite my alcove. I had forgotten to pull the blind again. It was dark outside and I looked at the reflection of myself in the bright computer room.

Or whatever kind of room it *really* was.

"They can't find us, Ray," said Ada. "You know that. We're onto a good thing. You know that too. Something that nobody can find out about. I blew a fair chunk of change on the job. Turns out Hollywood hits don't come cheap. And that's not counting the work I had to pull you off of to attend to this little matter."

I plugged myself in.

"They can't find us, Ray."

"I know that, Ada," I said. "That's why you had me kill Coke Patterson. Maybe you didn't know he was a DORL agent but you knew he'd found out too much and was going to spill it somewhere he shouldn't."

Ada drew on her cigarette. Now it was her turn not to do any speaking.

"And Ellis too," I said. "He'd been spooked. But he wanted to get out of Falzarano's protection and quick. Maybe he would have talked. Maybe he wouldn't. But there was too much of a risk of DORL getting their hands on him." I shrugged. "And besides, he was part of the job anyway. No harm, no foul. All I had to do was wait until he made his bid for freedom. Shame about the guard. I guess I had no option. I had to get in without being seen and deal with the problem of Emerson Ellis one way or another."

"We'll make a detective out of you yet, chief."

"Of course I don't know what happened to Vaughan Delaney, other than the fact he fell out of a building. But that's something people do. Maybe his good conscience got the better of him. The hell do I know?"

"You had to admit, it keeps everything tidy, Ray."

"I know that."

"A good night's sleep is what you need, Ray. Everything will look better in the morning."

"I know that too, Ada," I said, "and I also know that I can't do a damn thing about it."

Ada laughed. Three full loops. And then when she was done she said, "Good night, Ray."

And then I woke up and it was another beautiful day in Hollywood, California

ACKNOWLEDGEMENTS

The life and times of Raymond Electromatic owe a great deal to a great many people, and with a bit of luck I might even be able to remember enough of them to thank here.

Thanks to Tor Books: Miriam Weinberg, Diana Gill, Irene Gallo, Patty Garcia, and everyone else who has worked on my books. Thanks also to Paul Stevens, who started this whole thing, and to Will Staehle who continues to make me look really good on the shelf. Take a moment and close this book and look at the cover. That's all Will, under Irene's direction. Geniuses, the pair of them.

Thanks also to my agent, Stacia J.N. Decker of Dunow, Carlson & Lerner Literary Agency, whose advice, assistance, opinion, skills, talents, and above all friendship I not only value but call upon with a quite frankly terrifying frequency. You rock.

And thanks to my wife, Sandra, for support and

encouragement and advice and suggestions and ideas and infinite undying love. I love you!

ABOUT THE AUTHOR

Adam Christopher is a novelist and comic writer, and award-winning editor. The author of many novels, Adam is co-writer of *The Shield* for Dark Circle Comics and author of the official tie-in novels novels based on the hit CBS television show *Elementary*.

Born in New Zealand, Adam has lived in Great Britain since 2006.

THE SPIDER WARS TRILOGY

ADAM CHRISTOPHER

THE BURNING DARK

Captain Abraham Idaho Cleveland has one last mission before early retirement: decommissioning a semi-deserted research outpost on the edge of Fleetspace. Isolated and paranoid, Ida reaches out to the universe via radio, only to tune into a disturbing signal. Is the transmission just a random burst of static from the past—or a warning of an undying menace that threatens humanity's future?

THE MACHINE AWAKES

In this far future space opera set in the Spider War universe of *The Burning Dark*, a government agent uncovers a conspiracy that stretches from the slums of Salt City to the floating gas mines of Jupiter. There, deep in the roiling clouds of the planet, the Jovian Mining Corporation is hiding a secret that will tear the Fleet apart. But there is something else hiding in Jovian system. Something insidious, intelligent and hungry. The Spiders are near.

VICIOUS

V.E. SCHWAB

VICTOR and Eli started out as college roommates—brilliant, arrogant, lonely boys who recognized the same ambition in each other. A shared interest in adrenaline, near-death experiences, and seemingly supernatural events reveals an intriguing possibility: that under the right conditions, someone could develop extraordinary abilities. But when their thesis moves from the academic to the experimental, things go horribly wrong.

Ten years later, Victor breaks out of prison, determined to catch up to his old friend (now foe), aided by a young girl with a stunning ability. Meanwhile, Eli is on a mission to eradicate every other super-powered person that he can find—aside from his sidekick, an enigmatic woman with an unbreakable will. Armed with terrible power on both sides, driven by the memory of betrayal and loss, the arch-nemeses have set a course for revenge—but who will be left alive at the end?

"Supremely plotted and incredibly well-written."
The Independent on Sunday

KOKO TAKES A HOLIDAY

KIERAN SHEA

Five hundred years from now, ex-corporate mercenary Koko Martstellar is swaggering through an easy early retirement as a brothel owner on The Sixty Islands, a manufactured tropical resort archipelago known for its sex and simulated violence. Surrounded by slang-drooling boywhores and synthetic komodo dragons, Koko finds the most challenging part of her day might be deciding on her next drink.

That is, until her old comrade Portia Delacompte sends a squad of security personnel to murder her.

Now Koko is on the run in the sky-barges of the Second Free Zone—dodging ruthless eye-eating bounty agents dispatched by Delacompte and falling in with Flynn, a depressed local cop readying his nerves for a sanctioned mass suicide known as Embrace…

"Brutal, smart and wickedly funny."
Stephen Blackmore, author of *Dead Things*